"You Have Every R

Dev looked away.

"No." Megan's reply was barely audible. "I...tried. I wanted to hate you, but I couldn't. I didn't have the strength. All I could do was hurt."

"Because I'd drained all your strength," he said bitterly.

"No." The denial came again, nearly as soft as the first. "It made me stronger, knowing you needed me. At least...who I was...then."

"God, Meggie..."

Her body went suddenly taut. She'd heard those words, that tone, before, and the memory of when and where came flooding back.

"I know," he said, as if he'd sensed the change in her. "That's no excuse for what I did to you." He looked away again. "I was a bastard. I lied to you, hurt you unforgivably. I destroyed your youth, your trust and now I know I did something even worse. I destroyed your dreams."

She stared at him. "Dev," she whispered, unable to stop the tiny sound's escape.

Dear Reader,

Welcome to March! Spring is in the air. The birds are chirping, the bees are buzzing . . . and men and women all over the world are thinking about—love.

Here at Silhouette Desire we take love *very* seriously. We're committed to bringing you six terrific stories all about love each and every month of the year, and this March is no exception.

Let's start with March's *Man of the Month* by Jackie Merritt. It's called *Tennessee Waltz,* and I know you're going to love this story. Next, Naomi Horton returns with *Chastity's Pirate.* (How can you resist a book with a title like this? You just *can't!*) And look for books by Anne Marie Winston, Barbara McCauley, Justine Davis and new-to-Desire Kat Adams.

And in months to come, some of your very favorite authors are coming your way. Look for sensuous romances from the talented pens of Dixie Browning, Lass Small, Cait London, Barbara Boswell . . . just to name a few.

So go wild with Desire, and start thinking about love.

All the best,

Lucia Macro
Senior Editor

JUSTINE DAVIS

FOUND FATHER

SILHOUETTE *Desire*

Published by Silhouette Books New York

America's Publisher of Contemporary Romance

SILHOUETTE BOOKS
300 East 42nd St., New York, N.Y. 10017

FOUND FATHER

Copyright © 1993 by Janice Davis Smith

All rights reserved. Except for use in any review, the reproduction
or utilization of this work in whole or in part in any form by any
electronic, mechanical or other means, now known or hereafter
invented, including xerography, photocopying and recording, or in
any information storage or retrieval system, is forbidden without
the permission of the publisher, Silhouette Books, 300 E. 42nd St.,
New York, N.Y. 10017

ISBN: 0-373-05772-5

First Silhouette Books printing March 1993

All the characters in this book have no existence outside the
imagination of the author and have no relation whatsoever to
anyone bearing the same name or names. They are not even
distantly inspired by any individual known or unknown to the
author, and all incidents are pure invention.

® and ™: Trademarks used with authorization. Trademarks
indicated with ® are registered in the United States Patent and
Trademark Office, the Canada Trade Mark Office and in other
countries.

Printed in the U.S.A.

JUSTINE DAVIS

lives in San Clemente, California. Her interests outside of writing are sailing, doing needlework, horseback riding and driving her restored 1967 Corvette roadster—top down, of course.

A policewoman, Justine says that years ago, a young man she worked with encouraged her to try for a promotion to a position that was, at that time, occupied only by men. "I succeeded, became wrapped up in my new job and that man moved away, never, I thought, to be heard from again. Ten years later he appeared out of the woods of Washington state, saying he'd never forgotten me and would I please marry him. With that history, how could I write anything but romance?"

For Kris—

While it's true you weren't in my game plan, I wouldn't change the way it turned out for anything. You've taught me as much as I've taught you. Thanks for becoming "my kid"— and my friend.

One

"What do you think you're doing here, Cross? This is way out of your league."

Devlin Cross muttered the words to himself as he walked past the row of luxury cars to the wide, curved steps of California State Senator Harlan Spencer's house.

He shifted his shoulders beneath his coat. At least he hadn't had a problem deciding what to wear; the dark, well-cut suit was the only thing he owned even moderately close to the kind of clothes he knew he'd encounter on the other side of the heavy, carved oak doors. While his company was doing well, he himself wasn't out of the woods yet; his strained budget hardly ran to designer suits and silk ties.

He shrugged heading up the front steps. He hadn't wanted to come to this party to begin with, so if they didn't like how he was dressed, they could just throw him out; it certainly wouldn't break his heart. The only reason he was here at all was because he'd made the mistake of saying no when Frank Mason had asked if he was doing anything tonight, and the man now beside him had insisted. Adamantly.

"The senator likes your type," his current client had said. "Young, enterprising, running your own business, expanding. The American Dream, that's what rings his chimes."

Yeah, Dev thought glumly. That's me—the picture of the American Dream. Only mine turned into a nightmare.

The door opened for them as quickly as if it had been the electronic door of one of Mason's shopping centers. A butler, Dev thought in amusement. An honest-to-God butler. Oh, you *are* out of your league, Cross.

They went through the foyer, which was tiled in squares of black and white marble, to a large, elegantly appointed room he supposed would be called a parlor or drawing room. He wasn't sure; his experience didn't run to houses this size. He heard light, cheerful music, playing at just the right volume to be a backdrop for the conversations going on in the clustered groups of expensively dressed people gathered there.

Thirty seconds after he'd turned down Mason's offer of a "real drink," he found a glass of champagne pressed into his hand and the efficient waiter gone before he could protest. He wished, he thought as he watched Frank Mason make his way to the big, elaborate bar a few feet away in the corner of the room, that he had driven here himself. At least then he'd have the option of making a discreet—and early—exit. He smiled to himself at the image of his battered old Jeep amid all that automotive splendor outside.

He saw Mason pause beside a tall, statuesque blond woman in a dramatic dress of black and white shot with silver sparks. A metallic silver band slashed across one shoulder, dividing the black and white diagonally across the body to the hip, where it met with a matching band at the cuff of one long sleeve. The fabric clung subtly, emphasizing the long, slender lines of her body; in those heels she had to be five-ten, he figured. Five-eight without them.

And all legs, he thought, feeling a sudden spurt of awareness that startled him, so long had it been since he'd felt anything like it. Her hair was up in a precise French twist— An image of bright blue eyes beneath a tousled mop of short, sunlit blond hair suddenly shot through his mind; he quashed it with the ease of long practice.

Dev was startled when Mason lifted a hefty arm to gesture in his direction, and embarrassed when the man's words drifted back to him.

"—doesn't know anybody here, so take care of him for me, will you, honey?"

"Of course, Frank."

The words were smooth, practiced, as was the smile that curved full, perfect lips as the woman turned to look at him. Dev nearly dropped his glass.

For a moment, a brief flashing second, he thought he might be mistaken. But then he saw the widening of her eyes, the slight parting of her lips as she stared, and he knew it was true. Impossibly, heart-wrenchingly true.

Instinctively he took a step forward, toward the vision in the sparkling gown. The instant he moved, he saw the change overtake her, saw the smooth, emotionless expression come over her face as if it were a mask. That moment of shocked recognition might never have been, and as Mason took his drink from the bartender and started back toward Dev, she allowed the big man's arm at her elbow to guide her along with him.

"This is Dev Cross," Mason said as they came to a stop, introducing them. "Dev, Megan Spencer, the senator's daughter."

Dev couldn't seem to find his voice, but Megan seemed to be suffering from no such problem.

"Mr. Cross," she acknowledged with a regal inclination of her head. Her voice held the perfect combination of benevolent hospitality and distance; the hostess to a guest. And a stranger.

"Miss...Spencer?" Having found his voice at last, he couldn't help the questioning tone.

"Yes," she said firmly. "I see you have some champagne already...Mr. Cross. The buffet table is right over there, please help yourself. Ah, Cynthia, hello." She flagged down a passing woman, a rather predatory-looking platinum blonde. "Meet Mr. Cross. He's with Mr. Mason, and new here, so keep him...entertained, will you, dear? I have to see the caterers about the dessert table."

As smoothly as that she was gone, leaving Dev staring after her in shock.

"Well, hello there," Cynthia purred, eyeing Dev's tall, well-muscled length. He glanced at her somewhat vaguely, registering only how false that silver shade of hair looked, especially next to the rich, honey gold of the woman who'd just disappeared through a pair of double doors at the far end of the room. Only when he realized that Frank Mason was looking at him oddly did he yank his attention back to the pair before him.

"Well," Mason said curiously, "that's as close as I've ever seen Megan to being rattled."

"An unexpected guest does that, I imagine." Dev kept his tone carefully even.

"Oh, Megan's very good with *that* sort of thing," Cynthia purred, the implication clear that details like that were all her hostess was good at. "So, tell me, Dev—may I call you that?"

With a smothered sigh, Dev gave her a short nod. His eyes returned to the double doors across the room.

"What is it short for? Devereaux, or something romantic like that?"

"Devlin. Not romantic at all." Liar, he told himself. Sometimes, on the right lips, it was as romantic as hell.

"Oh, but I think it is!"

"You women," Mason said with a laugh, "always with your head in the clouds when a good-looking young st—er, man is around."

"Not Megan," Cynthia said too sweetly, "she's the most levelheaded person I know. The precise, efficient, perfect woman. There's not a romantic bone in her body."

Dev cringed inwardly. Cynthia, he thought, was getting on his nerves, nerves already strung tight from the unexpected jolt he'd just received.

"So—" she was purring again "—you're new here in Aliso Beach. Does your wife like it? Perhaps I could show her some of the local shops?"

As subtle as a bulldozer, he muttered silently. "No," he said shortly, without explaining any further. Past caring about appearing rude, he turned to Mason. "You wanted me to meet the senator?"

"Sure do. Come on, son, I'll introduce you."

"Excuse us," Dev said pointedly to the pouting Cynthia, and let the big man lead him away. He glanced over his shoulder one last time to the still-closed double doors.

Megan shut the library doors behind her and turned the lock with trembling fingers. Her heart was hammering so hard she thought it must be audible from across the room. She sucked in a long, deep breath and pressed her hands to her temples.

Why here? she moaned inwardly. Why now?

Don't be silly, she snapped in instant answer to her own useless plea, it wouldn't be any better anywhere else, or at any other time. She'd hoped, she'd even prayed, never to run into Devlin Cross again; but if it were to happen, she'd never in the world have thought it would happen here, in her own home.

What on earth was he doing here? He had to be the person Frank Mason had asked to bring at the last minute, someone connected with the Gold Coast project, he'd said. She'd said yes automatically, her ability to cope with last-minute changes the one source of pride she allowed herself. But all thought of being able to cope with anything had been blown to bits the moment she'd turned and found Devlin Cross standing there.

She didn't know how long she'd been there, sagging against the library doors, before she began to regain some fragment of control. She had to go back to the party, she thought. She'd done enough hiding from the world because of Devlin Cross. She drew herself up, stiffened her spine and squared her shoulders. She would go back, and if she saw him again, she would pretend it meant nothing to her. That she barely remembered him. That he had meant as little to her as she had meant to him. Not for anything would she let him know how badly the foolish little girl she'd once been had been hurt.

"Megan?"

Her head snapped around, a strand of honey-colored hair escaping the perfect twist.

"Oh! You startled me."

"Sorry, honey." The tall, imposing man from whom she had inherited her determined chin came into the room from the private door leading into his office. He crossed the distance between them, moving with long, youthful strides that belied his silver hair.

"Someone said you'd come in here, and the outer doors are locked. Are you all right?"

"Yes, Dad. Just . . . a little headache."

His concern was immediate. "Did you take something? Some aspirin?"

"I will. I'll be fine, really."

"You've been working too hard, haven't you? With this party and the speech at the awards banquet coming up, on top of everything else, you've been running like mad."

She drew in a deep breath to steady herself. "I'm fine."

"Well, you're going to slow down."

"I will. As soon as everything's caught up."

He looked at her for a long moment. "What would I do without you, Megan?"

"Scramble your schedule. Field your own phone calls. Write your own corny speeches. Serve hot dogs to the Orange County elite. Hire a cryptographer to decipher your notes—"

"Okay, okay," he said with a laugh. "I get the point. And haven't I always said you're indispensable?"

No, she thought suddenly, in an uncharacteristic rush of bitter remembrance. Once you said I was a naive child. But I left anyway, determined to prove you wrong, and only wound up proving that you were absolutely, exactly right.

With an effort she shook off the memory and the bitterness, and said lightly, "Except when I was fourteen and hit a baseball through the window of your new car."

He hugged her suddenly, fiercely. "Well, you *are* indispensable. And you were, even then."

"I love you, Daddy," she said suddenly, as if in atonement for her disloyal thoughts. She knew he'd never meant to hurt her, and she could hardly blame him for being right.

"I love you, too, honey." He backed up, holding her slender shoulders as he looked at her. "Oh, baby, you look so much like your mother tonight."

Megan's eyes flicked to the portrait over the mantel of the big fireplace. The woman who smiled gently down at her was lovely, and although Megan could see the resemblance in the luxurious color of her hair and the bright blue eyes, she knew there were differences as well. Catherine Spencer's gentle mouth had never tightened with temper, and her perfect nose didn't have the sassy, turned-up tip that met Megan in the mirror every morning. And above all, those eyes had never held the cool, cynical cast hers did. But she knew her father meant the words as a compliment, and she tried to accept as gracefully as she could.

"Thank you, Dad. You look rather impressive yourself." She reached to straighten his tie, as her mother always had.

"I'd better get back," he said briskly, following it with a grimace. "Frank Mason wants to thank me some more."

"Well, he should, the way you went to bat for him at the Coastal Commission meeting. You know that development of his would have taken forever to get passed if you hadn't."

"It would have gotten through eventually, once he finally dropped that private golf course idea in favor of a small state park. He'll get his hotel, and the Commission gets what they want, plenty of public access to the beach, lots of open space and low density. We don't want this area to wind up looking like Waikiki Beach." He smiled somewhat wryly. "But I can only take his gratitude in small doses."

"He *can* talk." Megan's mouth twisted slightly.

Her father chuckled. "Your restraint is admirable, dear. I know you've never really cared for him."

"I don't care much one way or the other," she corrected. She paused before she went on, and if her voice was a little tentative, her father didn't seem to notice. "Have you...met his guest yet?"

"Cross? Just briefly, before I came in here. He seems like a nice young man. Solid, if a bit quiet. His company has an excellent reputation. It's always good to have new businesses like that open up here."

Megan's breath caught in her throat. "Here?"

Harlan nodded again. "Cross opened a second office here in Aliso Beach a few months ago." He smiled. "Must be doing well, to afford the office rents. His partner's running the San Diego office, Frank said. Not a bad gamble, if they stay in good with Mason Development. All of their projects could keep a geological firm busy for a long time. The Gold Coast project alone will keep them hopping for months."

Meg felt a strange weakness in her knees. Dev had been here for months. Living in the same town, driving the same streets, breathing the same air—

"Megan, honey, are you sure you're all right? You're as pale as a ghost."

She felt her father's steadying arms again, but couldn't speak. A ghost. How appropriate that he should say that, for her past had certainly come back to haunt her tonight.

"I . . . I think I'll lie down on the couch for a minute or two. Perhaps I *am* just a little tired."

It was such a rare admission from her that Harlan didn't press for any reason why. "All right. And don't worry about anything, the caterers can keep things going."

He fussed for a few minutes more, and Megan endured it while wishing desperately to be alone. When at last he turned to leave, he switched off the light . Megan let out a long, harsh breath and lay there in the dark, staring up at the ceiling her not-yet-adjusted eyes couldn't see.

Devlin. *Here.* Oh, God.

With a terrible feeling of resignation, like that of a person trapped on a rocky shore watching a tidal wave's inexorable approach, she felt the memories swell upward out of the dark recesses of her mind.

Dev. Looking just the same, yet different. The rich brown hair still gleamed with golden highlights, his skin was still tanned from his work outdoors. And he was still tall enough that she had to look up at him, even in the heels that she wore tonight. But he somehow looked more solid now, not heavier, just more muscular, as if he had added the weight she'd always told him he needed in those long ago days. But the biggest change was in his eyes; the dark, haunted look that had so worried her then was gone. Only it had been replaced by an ancient-seeming weariness that seemed somehow much worse.

She had thought nothing could be worse than that haunted, driven look. It had struck a chord deep inside her young, innocent heart before she'd even known who he was. From the first time she'd seen him, those hazel eyes had burned a deep, aching spot in her heart.

She remembered it so well, that frozen instant in time. She'd nearly poured coffee all over the table the moment he'd looked up at her, managing a smile of thanks in spite of the fatigue that so obviously shadowed his eyes and carved deep lines into a face far too young to bear them.

She'd barely managed to write down his order, so fascinated had she been by the deep, husky sound of his voice and the strong, masculine planes of his face. When she'd gone to turn the order in to the cook, she had cornered Felice, the head waitress who had been at the coffee shop much longer than her own two weeks. . . .

"Dev?" The older woman's quick, dark eyes had immediately zeroed in on the man sitting alone in the booth in the farthest corner of the nearly empty café. "Yes, he's a regular, for a couple of years now. Just hasn't been in for a couple of weeks. Her eyes flicked to Megan, a teasing glint lighting them. "He is a hunk, isn't he? Interested?"

"No," Megan said hastily. "It's just . . . he looks so . . ."

"Yes, I know." Felice's considerable maternal instincts rose to the fore. "Tired, too thin—carrying a heavy load, that boy is. Got the weight of the world on his shoulders. Nice shoulders, though," she added, with another teasing look at Megan. "And the face ain't bad, either. Strong jaw, great mouth. Want me to introduce you?"

Megan flushed. "No. I just ... wondered. Besides, he's a little old for me, don't you think?"

Felice chuckled, the sound bubbling up from her ample girth. "I know you're only nineteen, girl, but don't make me feel even older than I am. And don't let his eyes fool you. He's probably only a couple of years on the shy side of thirty."

Megan looked over her shoulder, contemplating the man whose head was now bent over some papers scattered over the table he was seated at. From here, where she couldn't see those eyes, he did look younger. Something about the thickness of the brown hair, or the seemingly vulnerable nape of what was a strong, muscular neck, she thought.

"Does he always do that? Come in alone and sit back in the corner, with a pile of work?"

"Yep. Charts and figures and graphs. I don't know what he does, though." She shrugged. "I never really asked. He doesn't talk much, and I don't like to push."

"It would be hard to push someone with eyes like that," Megan said softly, barely aware of speaking out loud.

After that day, and for the first time since she'd talked her way into the job at the little diner, Megan found herself looking forward to her job with something more than just a determination to prove to both her father and Felice that she could do it, that she wasn't just a spoiled child who didn't know how to work. Each day she wondered if he'd be there, if he'd look at her and give her that brief smile, wondered if there would be any change in those tired, hollow eyes.

She even caught herself thinking about him at school. On the two days a week that she ran from class to class from dawn to dark, her schedule set up that way so she could work three days a week and weekends, she usually had no time to think about anything but keeping up with the hectic pace. Yet he still managed to creep into her thoughts. And for a moment she thought she was wearily confusing both her worlds when, pouring him his coffee one afternoon, she saw what was on the papers on the table.

"Something wrong?"

She blinked, and met his curious gaze. She glanced at one particular sheet again, as if to make sure it hadn't disappeared, or metamorphosed into a perfectly ordinary business letter or something. Then she looked at him again.

"Is that . . . a soil profile?"

He blinked, as if startled by the fact that she'd done something beyond say hello and take his order, all she'd dared trust herself to do until now.

"Yes," he finally said. "Of a core sample."

"Whew." She let out a relieved breath. He raised an eyebrow at her. "I thought maybe I was seeing things."

"Seeing soil profiles?" He looked at her quizzically.

She sighed. "I'm taking Physical Geography in school. Or," she amended ruefully, "it's taking me."

He smiled in sudden understanding. "Too much studying last night?"

It took her a moment to answer; that smile, unlike the automatic, courteous ones he gave her when she poured his coffee, was a genuine one, and the change it made in his face was incredible.

"Too much studying and not enough understanding," she said at last, returning his smile.

He seemed as taken aback by her smile as she had been by his, and it took him a moment to speak. "What school?"

"UCSD."

"UC San Diego?" The smile again. "I went there."

She glanced at the pile of papers spread out before him. "Still doing your homework?"

His gaze flicked to the papers, then up to her face. She knew he could see the corners of her mouth twitching. Then, incredibly, he laughed. Not a loud, boisterous laugh—more like a rusty chuckle—but it was a laugh nonetheless, and Megan was stunned by the way it sent shivers down her spine. He looked as surprised as she was to hear it.

"Let me guess," he said after a moment. "Professor Eckert?"

"You mean, it's not just me he's harassing? He's always been like this?"

The laugh again, better this time, although he looked just as bemused by it as before. "Let's say he has . . . very high expectations."

"I'm an artist, not a rock hound." She sighed glumly. "It wouldn't be so bad if I understood half of what he said. But by the time I look up the first five-syllable word he throws out, I'm three more behind. And I never did understand those." She pointed to the diagram. "I mean, I know what they're supposed to be, the layers—oops, I mean horizons—of soil and all, but all that 'B is transitional to C' stuff . . ." She trailed off with a disgusted shrug.

He smiled, a good one again. Then he flipped over a piece of paper with some figures scribbled on it and drew something on the back with quick, sure strokes. When he turned it toward her, she saw it was a column broken down into layers of varying thickness.

"If you're an artist, think of the horizons as colors," he said. He pointed to the bottom one. "This is, say, pure blue, the underlying rock, an unmixed color. The next one is . . . oh, blue-green, maybe. Still mostly blue, but different than the first because of the green. Then another blue-green, but this one's more green than blue. Then you get to a real green, without the visible blue."

She stared at it. "You mean each one is like . . . a step? A shading? Gradual change from one color to another?"

He nodded. "Only with soil, you add different elements instead of colors. Ash, silica, lots of things, depending on the climate and other conditions. And bingo, transition."

"So all that 'A being transitional to B' stuff just means that soil A is headed for soil B, and the subscript number just tells you how far it's gone?"

His smile widened. "Or blue is headed to green, if you prefer."

She stared at him. "But... that makes sense!"

His smile became a full-fledged grin. "That's because there wasn't a five-syllable word in it."

She eyed the papers in front of him again. "You do this voluntarily?"

He chuckled. "I get paid for it. I'm a geologist."

She stared at him. "Well, I suppose somebody has to be." She looked at the drawing that had made sense out of the chaos she'd spent so many weary hours on last night. "I guess I never really thought about it. Who pays you?"

He smiled at the ingenuous question. "Developers, builders. The government, sometimes." He shrugged. "They tell me what they want to build and where, I tell 'em if it'll stand."

The call from the kitchen that his meal was ready sent her hastily to pick it up, aware of all the time she'd spent at his table. When she came back with the plate, he looked up at her consideringly.

"You're really having trouble with Eckert's class, Meg?"

She knew her name was on the badge she wore, but she was still startled at how easily he used it, as if he'd been saying it for years. It took her a moment to answer him.

"He's going to blow my grade-point average to pieces."

"I..." He stopped, lowered his gaze, shifted the plate in front of him, toyed with the knife, then looked back at her again. "I could... help you a little, if you want."

And so it had begun, the hours spent together as he had coached her, prodded her, all with a tact and patience that amazed her. He never belittled her for her lack of understanding, never commented when she missed one on the endless lists of things she had to memorize. He just ran through it again, giving her some kind of memory trick, and after the first two weeks, the course material that had seemed incomprehensible began to fall into place.

The days had stretched into weeks, and even when it became apparent that she no longer needed his coaching, she was reluctant to call a halt to their meetings. He seemed to feel the same way, and as their conversations about her schoolwork grew shorter, their talks about everything else expanded. He told her about his own days at the beautiful University of California at San Diego campus, his work and all the places it had taken him.

She was amazed whenever she had time to think about it, that despite all the time they spent together, she knew so very little about him. He was twenty-seven—eight years' difference qualified him as an older man, she supposed—he was quietly handsome, and patient enough to tutor someone who had no knowledge of what was old hat to him.

He also had a way of making her feel as if she had accomplished some kind of miracle every time she made him laugh; each time that happened he looked so surprised it made her wonder what kind of life he led that made the simple gift of laughter so unfamiliar. She could never shake the feeling she had that he was trapped somehow, caught and held by something beyond his control.

She wanted to ask, to plead with him to let her help, as he had helped her, but she knew if she did she would get only that polite demurral she always got when she trod on ground that was too personal. It hurt, especially since she'd told him so much of herself, her dreams, hopes, disappointments, even the pain she still felt at the loss of her mother four years before. He'd held her then, for the first time, silently but fiercely. She'd felt him quiver with strain, as if he wanted to comfort her, yet wanted to escape.

He came occasionally to her small apartment to help her study. The first time, he'd glanced at the sketches on the walls, renderings of people, places, and many of animals. Some were framed neatly, others just tacked up in a scattering that somehow managed to look planned. They were all vigorous and dynamic, and he'd guessed their source easily.

"You're good."

He said it with no surprise, but as if he'd merely had something he'd already known confirmed. Meg wrinkled her nose in a way that made her suddenly seem even younger.

"Not yet, but I'm trying. Those are there to remind me how far I have to go yet."

"You'll make it, Meg."

She turned her gaze away from the wall to look at him, and once more surprised that hungry, longing look in his eyes, the look that always vanished so quickly she was never positive she'd really seen it.

She remembered with startling vividness the night he had come to help her study for her geography final, remembered the moment when she'd first realized what had happened to her. It wasn't a trumpets-and-flashing-lights realization, as she had always half expected. It had just been Dev bending to pick up the soda glass he'd used. When his jeans tightened over his strong thighs and tautly muscled buttocks, she'd felt a sudden rush of sensation.

Oh, Lord, she thought. It's finally happened. Her heart raced like a trip-hammer and heat flowed through her in a most amazing flood, and all just because Devlin Cross had moved a certain way. He must have read her look, because that night, for the first time, Meg was almost certain he was going to kiss her. But then he pulled away, making a sound that tore at her.

"Dev... ?"

"I'm sorry, Meg," he said hoarsely, backing away.

"No...please..." She stopped, catching her breath at the look that came over his face at the pleading note in her voice; it was an expression of pure anguish.

"Oh, God, Meg," he groaned. He stopped, swallowing tightly. "I've got to go."

With a jerky motion totally unlike his natural, graceful movements, he turned on his heel. He crossed the small room in two long strides and yanked open the door. At the last second, he looked back over his shoulder at her.

"You'll be fine, Meg," he said softly.

And then he was gone, leaving her staring at the door he closed carefully behind him. And wondering why those words had sounded so much like a farewell.

In the days afterward, while she wandered around in a daze with no idea of how she had done on the brutal exam, she found out why: apparently they had been just that, a farewell. Day after day passed, and there was no sign of him. Had something happened? Had whatever haunted those expressive hazel eyes caught up with him? Was he all right?

At last, as the second week neared an end, she made a decision. Taking a sheet of stationery, she wrote a few short words: *Dev—I got an A. Thank you. Meg.* And before she could change her mind, she wrote the address she'd found in the phone book for Cross Consulting on the envelope, marked it Personal and mailed it. Four days later, as she stood talking to Felice at the end of her shift, the older woman went silent, staring over Meg's shoulder.

"Don't look now, child, but here comes your handsome tutor. And he looks a little ragged around the edges."

He looked, she thought in dismay, terrible. His eyes were sunken, darkly shadowed, and he looked as if he'd dropped another ten pounds from his lean frame, weight he couldn't afford to lose. His hair was tangled, as if he'd run his fingers through it once too often, and his firm jaw was shadowed with stubble. He was wearing a pair of dark slacks, and a gray shirt that looked as if he'd worn it to bed. Except that he looked as if he hadn't slept in days.

He was just outside, turning his back to the glass doors now. He moved away suddenly, but after three strides, he stopped and came back toward the café. He halted once more in front of the doors, then turned his back on them yet again. His broad shoulders slumped, and one hand came up blindly, as if looking for some kind of support. It found the corner of the building, and he sagged a little against the prop.

"Go on, honey," Felice urged. "Before he loses that battle and leaves."

"Or wins it and leaves," she said, her voice taut. But she went, pulling the door open just as he straightened up, slowly, as if the weight of the world were truly on his shoulders. She stopped behind him, bracing the door so it closed quietly. She bit her lip, then took a deep breath.

"Dev?"

He went rigid, his shoulders snapping back as if she'd struck him. Moving as if in pain, he turned, still shoring himself up with that hand on the wall. And when, after a long, strained moment, he spoke, every bit of the misery in his eyes was in his voice.

"I tried, Meg," he whispered.

"Tried . . . what?"

"To stay away."

Her throat was painfully tight. "Why, Dev?"

"I . . ."

She recognized it, that start and stop of words. "What is it, Dev? What is it you keep trying to tell me?"

He tried again, but when he finally got the words out, she knew it wasn't what he had been going to say. "I...got your note. Congratulations."

"*You* deserve the congratulations. I never would have done that well without you." Her voice caught on the last words, and she swallowed tightly.

He shrugged, a sharp movement that spoke of the tension still drawing him tight. "You would have done all right."

"All right, maybe. But not an A. Thank you."

"You're...welcome." At last, as if the surface normalcy of the conversation had bolstered him, he lowered his hand from the wall. "I wanted... I thought maybe..." His other hand went to his hair again, to run through the heavy, finger-tangled thickness of it. "Would you like to go out and celebrate?"

The words came out in a rush, and once again she didn't know if he'd won or lost the inner battle he was fighting. It was this that made her hesitate even as her heart leapt at the thought of going out with him.

"You don't look like you feel like celebrating."

He gave a short, harsh, mirthless chuckle. "I know. Believe me, I know."

She studied him for a moment, wondering how much she dared say. At last she said, "You look like a man who's torn. Or trapped."

Something flickered in his eyes, something dark and pained. "Give the lady a medal," he muttered.

Meg felt as if a cold, metal claw had gripped her heart, and with every glimpse of his torment it tightened that grip. "Whatever it is...can't you let it go, just for a while? Please, Dev, give yourself some peace."

"What do you think I'm doing?" The words broke from him hoarsely, and there was no doubt that this time it was against his will. "Every time I come to see you... You're the only peace I've had..."

He stopped, turning away. Meg reached for him, touching his arm, forcing him with the gentlest of pressures to turn back to her. "I think... I knew that."

His eyes widened, and this time he made no effort to hide the pain. After a moment he let out a long breath. "I suppose you did." He shook his head slowly. "You're so wise sometimes. I need that wisdom, Meg. And other times, you're so young, so energetic..."

"And you need that, too," she whispered.

"Yes!" he hissed, as if that final admission hurt more than all the rest.

"Dev," she whispered, helpless to do anything but what she did then; she went to him, putting her arms around him and hugging him. And to her amazement, his arms came up and embraced her, pulling her tight against him.

"I have no right to this," he said brokenly, "but I'm going to take it. I don't seem to have a choice anymore."

She didn't know what he meant. She did know that it was all tied up in the things he'd never told her. That whatever was eating away at him had begun long before he'd met her. And she knew instinctively that she had made it both better and worse for him, although she didn't know how or why.

She knew all of this, but at this moment none of it mattered. All that mattered was that Dev needed her. He needed her now, desperately, and she found it impossible to care about anything else. And in that moment, she realised just how much she loved Devlin Cross.

She had worked desperately to lighten his load that night. She chattered about any- and everything, in the way she knew made him smile. She had insisted on champagne, even though she was too young to drink it—which hadn't stopped her from stealing a few sips from his glass—and kept his glass refilled until the bottle was empty. And on some instinctive level she had known, as he turned that last glassful so that he could drink from the spot her lips had touched, what was going to happen that night.

Was she seducing him? she wondered. Was this how a man went about it, concentrating solely on making his quarry smile, and not above using alcohol to loosen any inhibitions? To her amazement, she found she didn't care. The only thing important to her tonight was to wipe that haunted look from his eyes, to give him as much as she could of the peace he said he found with her....

Megan jerked herself out of the quagmire of remembrance, quashing the memory she never allowed to surface. She sat suddenly upright on the couch in the library. If you're going to remember, she told herself coldly, remember the morning after. Remember waking up alone. Remember realizing that after so sweetly, passionately making love to you, after being so exquisitely gentle in taking your virginity, Devlin Cross sneaked out in the middle of the night without a word. Remember being the little fool who was too stupid to see the signs. Who had been utterly naive enough to call his office....

"Cross Consulting."

Mrs. Harris, Meg had thought over the clatter of dishes in the coffee-shop kitchen, remembering that Dev had told her about the woman. "May I speak to Mr. Cross, please?"

"I'm afraid he's not in now. May I take a message?"

"I... Do you know when he'll be in?"

"I'm sorry, I can't really say." And then the woman with the kind voice spoke the words that shattered Meg's life. "If it's an emergency, I could give you a number, although he doesn't like to be disturbed when he's with his wife."

Two

Dev sat watching the sun gradually turn the rolling Pacific from black to gray, then through an impossible shade of pink to sparkling blue. It reminded him of a lesson he'd given once, likening horizons of soil to bands of color.

He shuddered as he sat on the knoll at the edge of the Gold Coast construction site, as much from the memory as from the early morning chill. He'd spent most of the night here, knowing he had little chance of any sleep. His mind had been churning like a rock polisher, but it didn't seem to be producing any smoothed edges; every thought was razor-sharp, slicing until he was amazed he wasn't bleeding.

He hadn't seen Meg again after that first stunned encounter, although he had to admit he hadn't waited very long before he'd made his own escape from the party. Mason hadn't understood why he wanted to leave the glittering gathering; he knew Dev didn't often have the chance to mingle with this kind of crowd.

"You work too hard, son," he'd said.

"That's why you hired us."

"Not to work twenty-four hours a day. Relax, enjoy yourself." He gestured at the roomful of people. "Lots of business contacts here, you know."

"I'll just count on you to keep us busy."

Mason laughed, and Dev had left in a cab a few minutes later. And had spent the entire ride to his rented apartment trying desperately to keep his mind out of old, worn channels. He'd thought the memories well buried, but he'd found out that night how fragile his hard-won peace had really been.

He didn't understand any of it. How could Megan Spencer, elegant, aristocratic daughter of state Senator Harlan Spencer, be Meg Scott? His Meggie, the one bright spot in too many dark, grim days? His Meggie, who had been more interested in all of her many enthusiasms, from her art to rock and roll, from homeless animals to baseball, than she had ever been in her appearance. His Meggie, who had been vital, alive, virtually crackling with energy, an energy he had so desperately needed then. His Meggie, with the sparkling, joyous blue eyes and the gleaming, tousled cap of blond hair, who bore so little resemblance to the sleek, perfectly groomed and unflappable woman who was Megan Spencer.

The little knot of pain that he'd lived with for so long tightened in his chest at the realization that she had lied to him, that he had never really known her at all. And immediately he steeled himself against it; he had no right to feel pain, he told himself in vicious self-condemnation. Not when it came to Meggie. Or Megan, he corrected himself. There was nothing of Meggie left in the woman he'd seen last night. Nothing left of the vibrant, effervescent girl he'd once known.

It had been that vibrancy that had drawn him to her then, that had made him look forward to the time he'd spent with her as he'd looked forward to little else in those days. He'd commiserated with her over the heavy load of taking all her classes on two days a week, and had found himself making a point of coming into the café on the days she was working, just to talk.

He'd told her about the company he'd begun three years before, over the advice of those who'd told him he was too young to go out on his own. She'd commiserated with him over that with a wry admission that that was something she'd heard from her father one time too often.

"He wanted me to stay at home and go to school there, or at least live in a dorm on campus. Even San Diego is too far for him," she'd said in disgust. "He thinks I'm a child."

In so many ways you are, he'd thought, even then knowing that he was using that very innocence, was feeding on that youthful energy and enthusiasm, needing so badly this one bright spot he'd found, desperate for the strength he no longer had. And she had given it, freely, seeming to sense that he needed something from her, even if she wasn't certain what it was.

She'd talked to him, answered his questions and made him laugh when he'd thought there was no laughter left in him. And after the first few times he'd avoided some of her more personal questions, she'd quit asking them.

He knew from the puzzlement that flashed in her eyes that she was confused by his reticence, but he was clinging to a fierce need to keep this one part of his life bright and free of the darkness that encompassed the rest. He needed this so badly, this one place he could come, this one person he could come to who knew nothing of his private hell, who wouldn't pepper him with concerned questions that he had no answers to, who didn't drown him in useless sympathy that did more for the giver than for him.

So he ignored the tiny voice that was telling him he was getting in over his head, and kept coming to the little coffee shop. And later, as his need for her grew, he gave in to the urge for more. By the time he realized he was out of control it was too late, and he'd wound up causing more damage than he could ever have imagined.

Now, as he sat on the bluff overlooking the Pacific, Dev closed his eyes against the pain. The sun was beginning to warm the air, and the smell of damp, freshly turned earth permeated the area. Dev knew it was impossible, but his weary mind kept finding a hint of gardenia in the air, sweet and exotic amid the rest.

As if he'd suddenly developed a penchant for self-torture, he inhaled again, as if searching for that rich fragrance. He closed his eyes, and his imagination supplied the scent easily, stronger now, honeyed and evocative. So evocative that his body reacted with a fierce suddenness that nearly left him breathless.

The memory of that sweet perfume was close, intoxicating, painful. As close as if he were wrapped in the dress that had been scented with it. As intoxicating as if she were here, with it rising from her heated skin. As painful as it had become, weighted down with remorse and heartache.

He groaned, rolling over on his side and drawing his knees up against the pain. He'd never meant it to happen, never intended it for a second. He'd been certain he could maintain his distance, certain he had bludgeoned his body into understanding that his need for her company was worth the price it was paying. That was the only reason he'd let himself go to see her after he'd gotten her note; he'd thought he was back in control.

He'd never forgotten the slightest detail of that night, and refusing to look at them for six years had done nothing to dim the memories. He had to look at them now, he thought, or he'd just lie here all day in a crippled little ball, waiting to be found by the workmen who would be arriving at the site soon.

Guilt flooded him the moment he opened that locked, sealed door in his mind. She had deserved so much better, deserved more than to waste her time on him—deserved more than to have her first time be with a man who was stealing something precious from her and giving her nothing in return. . . .

He had wanted to tell her about his marriage that night. He'd meant to tell her, just as he had countless times before. Then Meg had looked up at him, her clear blue eyes alight, so different from the grim, bleak looks he'd been living with for so long, and he knew he couldn't do it. Not yet. He needed her too much, needed her unshadowed joy, her liveliness and spirit. He would have to reveal the truth soon, but not yet.

When he'd taken her home so she could change out of her waitress uniform, he'd never expected the transformation she achieved; it left him breathless. She had put on a soft, knit dress instead of her usual jeans or pants, and it clung to her slim, graceful curves fluidly. It was a deep shade of teal, and it turned her eyes the same vivid color. Matching high-heeled sandals curved her long legs deliciously, and a simple gold necklace and earrings glowed softly. She'd swept her hair back on one side with a golden comb, baring one small ear and the delicate curves of jaw and neck. He'd always thought that someday, when she was a little older, she would set the world on its ear with her beauty; tonight he knew that someday was here.

"Meggie," he said, stunned; it was all he could manage.

"Thank you," she replied, reading in his eyes everything he couldn't say.

The moment lasted only as long as it took him to recognize the look that was glowing in her eyes; it was the same hunger he knew so often shone in his, and he began to wonder if he wasn't making a very large mistake. Her alone, and himself alone, he could handle; both of them together, he wasn't so sure about. The thought of what would happen if the two separate flames they'd been playing with ever flared out of control at the same time shook him to the core.

She was in rare form that night, energy rippling out from her so strongly that he was a little surprised it wasn't visible, like the bubbles rising in the champagne she'd insisted on; for him, she said, although she wouldn't mind sneaking a sip when the waiter, who'd eyed her youthful appearance suspiciously, wasn't looking. It would have taken a much stronger man than he was at the moment to resist her.

As she sat there, so alive, he slid his hand across the table to cover hers. It was another of many such quick, casual caresses that had become common for both of them, as if they were both rebellious children tempting fate by playing with matches. He knew it, but couldn't seem to stop, and he didn't know what to say to stop her. It couldn't hurt, he assured himself, as long as he stayed in control.

Tell her now, he'd ordered himself then, tell her before it goes any further. Before you drink any more of this damned champagne. Before you get up from this table. Because if you don't, it's going to go further, fast. But he couldn't find the words.

He soaked in her energy, feeding on it, letting it nourish his battered heart and soul. He felt the by now familiar qualm, the ghastly sensation that he was no more than a parasite, draining the life and animation from her because he had none left of his own. But he couldn't seem to stop, and gave himself over to the event, for that was what she made of it—an event, an adventure, a tour de force of gaiety and exhilaration. She taught him things he'd long forgotten, how to laugh at nearly nothing, how to find beauty in something as simple as the rose at their table and how it felt to look forward with joy instead of dread.

And when at last, as the clock began at the bottom of its progression of chimes once more, he took her home and entered her small apartment, it seemed inevitable that he would kiss her good-night.

By the time he realized what he'd done, that he'd taken those two, separate flames and recklessly thrown them together, it was too late. The moment his lips had touched hers the flames had taken hold, leaping, twisting, enveloping them both with a speed that spoke worlds about the parched tinder they found to feed upon.

He tried to stop, to pull back, but Meg, with a quiet little sigh, had gone soft in his arms, her lips warm and pliant against his, and he was lost. He felt her sag against him, the heat of her searing him through the soft, clinging cloth of the dress that had stunned him into the realization that his little gamine was a soft, luscious woman, taking his breath away even as she made him feel a little less a cradle robber for all the erotic images that had been haunting him since he'd met her.

"Dev," she breathed, and as she parted her lips for the sweet whisper of his name, his tongue slipped between them, stroking, teasing, feathering over her with the lightest of caresses. Almost at once, as if she'd never even thought of denying him, she opened for him, luring him into the honeyed depths of her mouth without even trying.

He tasted her, traced the even ridge of her teeth, then plunged deeper. When her tongue flicked tentatively over his, so quickly he was barely sure of it, heat burst from somewhere deep inside him and he felt an odd weakness in his knees. When she did it again, more definitely now, bolder, the last of his strength left his legs in a rush, as if to make room for the new flood of heat and sensation that was cascading through him.

They went down to the floor in a tangle, Dev cushioning her with exquisite care as he lay down beside her on the shag rug. He never broke the kiss. He couldn't; he'd never tasted anything so sweet, so beautifully, preciously sweet as this woman.

"Meg," he gasped finally, tearing his mouth away, "we've got to stop. I can't—"

His words broke off sharply as she lifted her mouth to his again. The conflagration blazed up anew, and the message that had been trying to get through to his pleasure-drugged mind was seared to ashes. He'd wanted this for so long, he'd fought it for just as long, and he couldn't seem to care that after all his battling, he'd lost the struggle. All he cared about was Meg, and easing the driving ache she caused in him, giving his body the release it was demanding. The release it wanted with her, only with her.

"Meggie," he said on a gulping breath, "please, help me, we can't do this...."

His words faded away as she trailed a line of soft, hot kisses along his jaw. She twisted in his arms, pressing herself against him, murmuring his name in a soft, wanting tone that fired blood already near to boiling. He was careening out of control and he knew it, he just couldn't quite remember why he'd once been so determined that this would never happen. He couldn't seem to remember anything except this, this raging fever, this consuming need and the feel of Meggie in his arms.

And then they were clawing at each other's clothes with a desperation that stunned him. He'd never been like this, and he knew even the long stretch of enforced celibacy couldn't account for this fury. He groaned, low and harsh as he bared her body to his heated gaze, to his searching hands. He touched her with reverence, stroking silken skin, then lifted his hands to cup the feminine curves of her breasts. His groan was throttled, a choking sound of near agony as he resisted the urge to take her this instant, without preamble, fiercely, hotly and much, much too fast.

Meg was pushing away interfering cloth, and her fingers brushed over him, inadvertently stroking naked flesh already hard beyond bearing. A fierce, electric charge jolted him, a choking gasp broke from deep in his throat, and convulsively, helplessly, he pressed himself against her hand.

"Dev? Did I hurt you? I..." She trailed off, but there was an odd note in her voice that somehow penetrated the thick haze of pleasure that had clouded his mind. Hurt him? God, she'd about sent him flying out of his skin with the merest of touches, and she thought she'd hurt him?

"No, Meggie." It came out on a shudder.

He heard her sigh of relief, then sucked in a searing breath as her hand began to move in a tentative caress. Something about her question and that tentativeness got through to him then.

"Meggie . . . you've never . . . done this, have you?"

She mumbled something he couldn't, but didn't need to hear; her furious blush was his answer. He should stop, he told himself, but his champagne-fogged mind couldn't come up with a reason why that could convince his hotly aroused body.

"Dev," she whispered, "please...it doesn't matter. I want it . . . and I want it to be you."

"Ah, Meggie," he said with a groan.

He knew it was too late, he had to have her. But he would make it good for her, he promised. He knew, from the way she shivered beneath his slightest touch, that he could. What he hadn't known was that in trying to make it perfect for her, he would find himself climbing to heights he'd never known. Never in his life had he known anything like the feel of Meggie in his arms, the sweet, innocent sensuality of her response, or the way her tender flesh first resisted him, then

welcomed him, surrounding him with a searing heat that
wrung a shuddering cry of her name from his throat....

He nearly echoed that cry now as he got shakily to his
knees on the scrub-covered bluff. He hadn't felt like this
since the morning he'd walked into his office the day after
he'd left Meg and found out that she had called...and what
Beverly Harris had told her.

"I had to leave her," he muttered desperately, staring
unseeingly at the wavering foam of the surf line. It had been
the right decision, the *only* decision. Look at how she turned
out, he told himself. She's beautiful, confident, poised. She
fits her world perfectly, the flawless political daughter.

A pang struck him as he remembered Meggie's determination never to be just that, the perfect political daughter.
She loved and admired her father, but his world wasn't hers,
she'd told him all those years ago. Yet here she was, playing the charming, socially correct hostess for him, and, if
what Frank Mason had said later was true, acting as his
glacially efficient aide.

But where was Meggie amid all that perfection? he wondered. Where was the energy, the vitality, that vibrant,
crackling something that had saved him? Was it still there,
buried beneath Megan's elegant exterior? Or had he drained
it all away and left her nothing but the polished shell he'd
seen last night?

God, all the times he'd thought of her, through all the
months he'd spent unsuccessfully searching for her, he'd
never thought of her like this. He'd always pictured her
happily using her artistic talent somewhere, satisfied with
that, as he'd known Meggie would be.

Unsuccessfully searching for her. It hit him with the force
of a blow, the delayed realization that he had, accidentally,
found her at last. That he could, at last, do what he had
never been able to: explain. That he could rid himself of at

least that much of his horrible guilt, that he could tell her why he'd had to leave her, why he'd never told her he was married.

He scrambled to his feet and ran, a little unsteadily, to his battered black Jeep. It was the same one he'd driven when he and Meg had been together. He'd been financially unable to replace it with a newer one, but he wasn't sure he would have even if he could have afforded to; Meggie had ridden in that passenger seat, enjoying the airy openness of the Jeep, loving the way the wind tossed her hair.

He started the vehicle and headed off the construction site back onto the Pacific Coast Highway. He needed a shower and a shave and fresh clothes before he confronted Meg. There was nothing he could do, he knew, about the dark circles shadowing his eyes.

He pulled into the garage of the Park Aliso apartments, parking the Jeep in his spot between two BMWs, and smiling wryly at its incongruous appearance next to the elegant sedans. He hurried into the small apartment, anxious now to get to Meg, to talk, to—as he'd never had the chance before—make her understand. And forgive? He tried to quash that thought as it formed. There was little chance of that, and he couldn't stand any more dashed hopes.

He took the stairs two at a time. He had rented this place when he and Jeff Russell, his business partner, had decided this job was worth opening an office here; Dev hadn't wanted to drive back and forth from San Diego to Aliso Beach every day. He'd told himself that what Mason was paying them justified moving to the elite coastal town, at least temporarily. And had refused to even consider that he'd done it because the wide-eyed sprite who had saved his sanity had lived here.

He hadn't known she still did, he rationalized now. And he hadn't chosen this particular apartment complex because she had once told him of spending hours at the tide pools just below it, watching the sea creatures who lived there. Just like he hadn't gone down to the pools himself, clambering over the rocks, picturing her there, a little blond whirlwind, energy virtually crackling around her.

He shut the door and tossed his jacket and keys down on the small table that sat just inside the door. The rent was, he thought, ridiculous for a place that had him sleeping in a small alcove off the living room, but he gathered that, for this town, it was considered reasonable. It was also furnished, another rarity here except for the beach rentals that went for more in a week than he was paying in a month.

He barely noticed the rather austere interior of the apartment. It didn't bother him; it was much like his own place anyway, utilitarian and pared to the essentials. He spent so little time here that he thought of it only as practical. And if Jeff told him he had nothing personal in his home because he was afraid to have anything personal in his life, well, his partner was entitled to his opinion.

It was just easier that way, Dev told himself as he showered and shaved. He didn't have time for anything but the basics. Jeff frequently told him that was intentional, too, but he shoved that thought out of his mind as well, with only a passing thought that he'd been doing a lot of shoving in the last few hours. Ever since, in fact, the tall, elegantly poised blonde in the sparkling dress had turned, and he'd found himself facing the woman who'd haunted his dreams for six years.

Megan was headed for the backyard when the doorbell rang. She knew that Mrs. Moreland had just gotten back from doing the weekly grocery shopping and was busy putting everything away, so she called out to the housekeeper that she would get it, and reversed her direction.

When she opened the door to Dev, she just stood there, staring. She couldn't seem to help it. And even though he had come here, he seemed as stunned as she felt. It was as if neither of them had truly accepted the truth of their encounter last night.

"Meggie," he whispered at last, as if barely aware he spoke aloud.

She stiffened, forcing herself to ignore the little shiver that went through her at the once beloved nickname. "Megan," she corrected formally.

The light went out of his eyes as if she'd dowsed it with ice water. "Sorry. I forgot it's not Meg anymore." One brow lifted as a corner of his mouth quirked in a joyless, off-center smile. "And not Scott anymore, either, is it? No wonder I couldn't find you."

He had looked for her? The shock of the idea made her voice sharp. "Scott was my mother's maiden name."

"I didn't realize your rebellion ran so deep as to dump your father's name."

"I didn't 'dump' it," Megan snapped. At a sound from behind her, she quickly stepped outside and pulled the door shut. "My father happens to be very well known, and on the Board of Regents of the University of California. I didn't want any special treatment just because I was his daughter. I—"

She broke off abruptly, angry at herself. Why was she explaining to him, as if he had a right to know? She had nearly told him her true name back then, more than once, but she hadn't wanted to risk the possibility that he, like so many, might treat her differently because of who her father was. And it had been a minuscule omission, compared to his.

Perhaps she *should* have told him, she thought acidly. Then maybe she wouldn't have been left in shattered pieces, trembling violently under the force of bitter betrayal as she clutched a cold, impersonal phone receiver in rigid hands.

"I don't owe you any explanations," she said tightly. "I don't owe you anything."

"No. You don't."

"If anyone owes anyone, it's you. You're the one who conveniently forgot about fidelity."

Her tone was biting. He lowered his eyes, as if fascinated by the intricate interlocking patterns of the expensive tile of the porch, but Megan knew he wasn't really seeing them when he went on softly.

"I . . . tried, Meg. I really did. I tried to stay away. And then . . . that night, I tried to stop. I told you we had to stop, that we couldn't—"

"You tried?" Fury made her voice low and harsh. "Did you ever think of trying the one thing that would have worked? Two simple little words, that's all. 'I'm married.' "

He sucked in a short, sharp breath. "I started to tell you, a hundred times."

She knew it was true, she'd long ago made sense out of those odd starts and stops of words that had come so often. But the knowledge hadn't eased her pain, nor did it cool her wrath now.

"So, tell me, Dev," she said with icy casualness, as if they were truly just recent acquaintances, "does your wife like Aliso Beach? Or did you conveniently leave her behind?"

He winced, and she saw his hands clench convulsively. "Meg, I know you're angry, and you have every right, but please . . . Will you just listen to me? I want to explain."

"It's a little late for that, isn't it?" Later than you'll ever know, she added bitterly to herself.

"Much too late," he agreed softly, surprising her. "But will you listen, anyway?"

"Please, spare me the 'my wife didn't understand me' bit, at least."

"It . . . was never that."

"However bad it was, I'm sure it was worse for her."

Dev drew in a deep, shaky breath. "It was. Much worse."

Megan was surprised by the admission. Then she again heard the sound that had made her close the door, this time drifting around the house from the backyard. She tensed.

"I don't see any point in this," she ground out. "Just go, will you?"

He winced at her sharp, grating tone. He let out a long, pained breath. "All right," he said, his gaze lifting to meet hers.

Megan saw with a shock that his eyes were as haunted as she had ever seen them. That shock was tinged with self-disgust as she realized that they also pulled at her in the same old way. As if he realized what he was revealing, a shutter came down in the hazel depths and he stiffened.

"I'll go," he said levelly, "but not before I tell you something. I know there's nothing I can say to undo what I did to you, Meg, but—"

"Megan," she repeated, hating the reminder of the fool she had been. At her insistent tone his jaw tightened.

"Megan, then." The rigidness of his voice was at odds with the pure emotion of his words as he went on. "I had no right to take what I took from you. I lied to you, and I hurt you. But I can't change that. Nothing can. I can only tell you why, and hope you can understand."

"Understand that you committed adultery with me? Believe me, I understand that." She shivered, wrapping her arms around herself. "Does your wife understand?"

"My wife," Dev said very carefully, "is dead."

Megan stared at him. "What?"

The words came quickly then, in choppy, staccato bursts, like automatic weapon fire. "She died five years ago. A year after we...after I left you. She had been in the hospital ever since she was hit by a drunk driver. It happened a year after we were married."

Megan stared, her mind racing as the words sank in. "A year after—"

"She was in a coma."

Meg's breath caught. "You mean she was...while you and I...?" She trailed off, shuddering; the idea was tremendously disturbing.

"Yes," Dev said bluntly.

Megan recoiled in revulsion, but the feeling died a quick, squeezing death at his next words.

"She was in a coma for three years."

Megan gasped. "Oh, God. Oh, my God."

"It had been two years, and I was...going under, when I met you."

It all came back, rushing into place like the last missing parts of some puzzle she'd thought she never could solve. Dev's haunted eyes, the lines of exhaustion grooved into a too-young face, and the sensation she'd so often had that he was fighting himself.

"I know that doesn't make it right," Dev said, still in that painfully careful tone. "And if guilt was the price for what I did, then you can be sure I've paid it every day of my life since. But there's something you need to know, to believe."

He took a breath, as if he needed to steady himself. It wasn't entirely successful, because even through her shock, Meg heard the thickness of emotion in his voice.

"I never meant to hurt you, Meg."

She was so stunned by what he'd told her, she couldn't even find her voice. The silence stretched out for a long moment, then his face hardened. He nodded once, short and sharp, as if in acceptance of her silence as her answer. He turned and started down the steps. Then he stopped and looked back at her.

"I know it doesn't matter to you," he said, not bothering now to hide the pain in his voice, "but I never would have made it without you."

And then he was gone, leaving Megan staring after the familiar black Jeep as he drove away. Something was twisting inside her, something with viciously sharp edges that dug and sliced. Dear God, she thought. A *coma*. for three years. Poor Dev. No wonder he had looked so worn, so ragged. No wonder she'd sensed that he was caught in a trap with no escape.

But why hadn't he told her? Had he thought she wouldn't understand? Had he thought she would have wanted nothing to do with him? It wouldn't have mattered, not if she'd known. Of course, it would have changed how she felt; she would have known she could never let it become a physical relationship—

That jagged thing inside her sliced deeper. Was that why he hadn't told her? Because he'd known she would never have made love with him? She cringed away from the thought even as she acknowledged her anger that it still hurt, after all this time.

She'd sworn she was through with pain when it came to Devlin Cross. He'd walked out of her life, and out he was going to stay. It was only a fluke that they'd crossed paths again—that had been clear by his look of shock when he'd seen her.

But he'd said he'd looked for her. After his wife had died, she supposed, since he certainly hadn't come back to her in the six weeks she had spent in her tiny apartment, waiting and praying for just that. And she supposed that should make her feel better. If she believed it, that is; of that she wasn't certain. But if it *was* true, he hadn't found her. Not that it was his fault, she realized. Meg Scott had been an illusion, an invention that had died along with her silly dreams.

She heard the sound from the yard a third time, a light, happy trill of laughter, and realized none of it mattered, anyway. She had needed Dev then, not a year later. She had needed him the morning she'd woken up alone after giving her virginity to him. She had needed him when she'd learned the price she was to pay for that night, when she'd learned the news that had struck the final blow to the naive girl she had once been. She had needed him when she'd had to face her father with the truth.

She had needed him when his son had been born.

Three

Dev stood on the hilltop, watching the heavy equipment moving across the construction site. The cool breeze off the Pacific stirred his thick hair, the brilliant California sun glinting on the gold strands among the brown. It was a crystalline winter day, with Catalina Island sitting long, sharp and clear just off the coast, and the smaller, lower shadow of San Clemente Island farther out to the south, visible on this day that was gloriously free of the haze that usually kept it hidden.

He looked out over the land that spilled in gentle, rolling knolls down to the Pacific, his quick eyes picking out the stakes marked with flags of various colors. This was going to be, he thought, a beautiful place.

He'd seen the designs and the artist's renderings, and he liked what Mason was doing here. Mason would get his ocean-view hotel, his shops and commercial area, while the people of the region would get a small yet impressive coastal park, complete with bike and jogging paths, picnic areas, parking and stairways down to the beach. No wonder Harlan Spencer was working with Mason so closely on this; it was going to be a showcase for his district and for the already elite town of Aliso Beach.

Dev wearily forced his mind away from thoughts of Meg's father, which naturally led to thoughts of Meg. She'd made herself quite clear yesterday; silence sometimes spoke volumes. He wasn't sure what he'd expected her reaction to be, but he couldn't deny he'd had hopes of something more positive.

He saw the long, dark sedan pull up to the construction trailer below him, but didn't pay much attention as he headed that way, slapping his hard hat idly against his leg. He was calculating where they would take the core samples for the next area to be graded.

He'd spent a lot of time concentrating—or trying to—on his work, but as a distraction it wasn't working very well. The memories were too strong, too overwhelming—from the old images of a vivacious, sparkling Meggie, to the newest, of a cool, refined woman who had little of the verve Meggie had had in such abundance. And little of her compassion or capacity for forgiveness.

Dev started down the last hill, wondering if his client had calmed down yet. When Mason had arrived this morning to find one of the dozers broken down, delaying the grading until a replacement part could be found, he had erupted into an abrasive tirade about the incompetence of the foreman in charge. He'd gotten on the site PA system and had blared out a demand that the man report to him immediately.

Dev had kept his eyes averted, sorting through a pile of papers on the desk he had in the trailer with much more concentration than the task needed. He had just picked up a piece of scratch paper covered in Mason's nearly indecipherable scrawl—the only word he could read looked like *flyash*—when Mason turned on him.

"What the hell are you doing with that?"

Dev blinked, startled, as the man grabbed the piece of paper out of his hand. "I just found it here—"

"Never mind. Just forget it." Mason crumpled the paper and stuffed it into his pocket, then turned as the unlucky foreman came in the door.

Dev had made a quick exit from the construction trailer as the argument began between the two men. His nerves were stretched far too tightly already without playing referee in another of his client's battles. Mason was starting to get on his nerves, Dev thought. These kinds of delays weren't at all unusual on projects of this size; he'd worked on enough of them to know that. But Mason seemed to blow up at the slightest problem, and it was wearing at best.

But when Dev got to the trailer now, it was obvious that Mason was at least hiding any residual irritation. He wore a wide smile as he approached the car that had come to a stop behind Dev's Jeep.

Dev stopped dead himself when the sedan's back door opened and a tall, silver-haired man got out. His breath caught in his throat as the driver's door swung open and one slim, curved, stocking-clad leg emerged, followed by a second. Then she was there, dressed in an elegant beige silk suit, her hair pulled back in a tidy chignon, baring delicate ears adorned with glowing pearl earrings. On her feet, impractically for the location, were darker tan high-heeled pumps.

They were explained the moment Dev saw her face; she hadn't known they were coming here. If she had, he thought sourly, he was sure she wouldn't have come. She would have found something else to do, anything else, and made someone else play chauffeur to her father.

Coming out of his daze, he shook the hand proffered by Harlan Spencer, trying not to notice how Megan's slender hands were tightly clenched on her purse; there would be no offer of a hand in greeting from her.

"Nice to see you again," Harlan said sincerely. Then he waved an arm at the site. "So, what do you think of Frank's undertaking here?"

Dev gathered himself to answer, looking away from that perfect, expressionless face. Megan might be more classically beautiful now, but it was a cold beauty without the life and verve that his Meggie had had.

"Impressive."

"Yes," agreed the senator. "It will be. A lot of work to be done, though."

Dev shrugged. "Better than no work."

The senator laughed. "I'd like to have you on my staff," he said. "Men of few words are a rarity in politics."

"Well, Dev is definitely that." Frank Mason clapped Dev on the shoulder heartily. "Never says two words when one will do. Sometimes I think he prefers dealing with rocks over people."

"Rocks don't talk as much," Dev said dryly.

Spencer laughed again. "I suppose not. And you're right, it is better than no work." He eyed Dev for a moment. "Frank tells me you work harder and longer than any two men he knows."

Dev shrugged again. "Necessity."

One silver brow rose. "Problems?"

"Short money blues. Nothing new." He wasn't about to discuss the reasons he'd had to put in five years of eighteen-hour days just to get out of the hole he was in. Especially with Meggie—Megan—standing there.

The senator's brow furrowed. "But I understood you've expanded, opened a second office here in Aliso Beach."

"The problem was . . . personal. The business is fine."

Only the tiny sound she made told him Megan was listening at all. His gaze flicked to her face, and he sensed her eyes dart quickly away, even behind though they were hidden the dark sunglasses. He knew she was remembering all the other times when he'd avoided any questions that trod on personal ground. Did it make any difference to her, to know why he'd done what he had? Had she forgiven him at all?

He tried to take heart from the realization that she wasn't quite as icily composed as he'd assumed, but somehow he couldn't find any comfort in the thought. The only emotions he'd seen in her so far were anger, shock and pain, all of which added another layer to the already heavy load of guilt he'd carried for a long time.

"So, let me show you around," Frank said expansively, reaching for a hard hat labeled Guest from the stack by the trailer.

"We don't have much time," the senator said, "but I'd like to see where the park is going in." He glanced to one side. "Megan?"

"No, thank you," she said stiffly. "I'm not dressed for clambering around in the dirt. I'll wait in the car."

Dev said nothing. Looking at Megan's stiff, unyielding posture told him there was nothing left to say. It had made no difference to her at all to know the truth about why he'd done what he'd done. Dev turned and walked away with the other two men without a word.

Frank Mason's enthusiasm was palpable, and if Dev thought it a bit extreme, he didn't say so. Yes, this was going to be a beautiful development, and yes, it would benefit both the citizens and the local business owners, but the big man seemed to be working awfully hard to sell to someone who'd already bought, and Dev was glad when at last he began to wind down.

When they reached the area set aside for the park, the senator asked about the markers with their various colored flags. "Grading markers," Mason answered gruffly. "Be ready to start as soon as Dev, here, quits stalling and gives me the go-ahead."

Harlan looked at Dev, who winced inwardly. He'd gotten used to Mason's brusque manner, but somehow he didn't like it in front of Megan's father.

"Stalling?" Harlan asked.

"Waiting for soil reports."

"Oh." Harlan smiled then. "Must be like waiting for staff reports. Take forever, but you can't make a move without them."

"Yes, sir," Dev said, surprised at the relief he felt. As if it would make a difference what Megan's father thought of him. Then he glanced at Mason. "Literally can't make a move without them."

"I know, I know," Mason muttered.

Harlan said to Dev, in a tone that clearly moved the conversation away from business, "Frank tells me you graduated from UC San Diego."

Frank talks too much, Dev thought as they started walking again, but he only nodded. If he'd had any doubts as to whether Meg had told her father who had driven her from San Diego, he knew now for sure; Harlan would hardly have been so friendly had he known.

"Megan started school there."

Dev's head came up, his shoulders tensing. "Oh?" he said, voice carefully neutral.

"Yes." Harlan shrugged, as if the subject were negligible. "She had this crazy idea about becoming an artist...."

Dev's forehead creased. *Had?* "Was it? Crazy, I mean?"

Harlan raised a brow, as if wondering at Dev's unexpected interest, but he answered easily enough. "Oh, she has a little talent—inherited from Catherine, my late wife, I suppose—but that's not the kind of field I wanted to see her in.''

A little talent, Dev thought numbly, remembering the vivid pictures that had hung on her walls, the sketches she'd always been doing, capturing her subject in swift, sure strokes of her pencil, pen, charcoal or whatever was at hand. He remembered too well one in particular, a quick charcoal portrait that was hidden away in his closet somewhere, where he didn't have to look at it and see everything that it told him about himself, and about her.

"She didn't—" He swallowed and tried again. "She didn't finish at San Diego?"

"Oh, no. She went to the university right here in Irvine, and graduated with honors."

"But not in art." Dev knew the answer even as he said the words.

"No, in business. She saw the light about that, at last." Harlan frowned, as if remembering something unpleasant. Then he brushed it off and said cheerfully, "I must say, it's a red-letter day for a parent when your child admits you were right all along."

"Well, you ought to be proud of her," Mason put in expansively. "She runs that office of yours like a drill instructor. I could use her—maybe things would stay on schedule around here."

Dev was barely listening; he could barely breathe. *Oh, God, Meggie, I'm sorry. So damned sorry.* He fought the knot that tightened his gut just as he fought the sudden stinging behind his eyes. He'd done this to her, destroyed her faith, her heart, her dreams . . .

"Excuse me," he said suddenly. "I . . . have to check on something."

He turned abruptly, not caring if the two men stared at him. But before he was out of earshot they were talking again, Mason's voice a bit strident as he said something about time schedules and investors.

Dev was almost back to the senator's car before he realized that was where he'd been heading. As he neared the car from behind, he could see Megan standing beside it, her arms crossed and resting atop the open passenger door as she stared out toward the ocean. She had taken off the sunglasses, and the wind had plucked free a few strands of honey-blond hair.

She jerked around as she heard him, and Dev came to a dead halt a bare two feet away, staring. Her cheeks were wet with tears. She was trembling, staring back at him, her eyes still brimming.

Dev didn't know what to do. That knot of pain tightened another notch, because he knew instinctively her tears were his fault. Again. Yet his heart leapt; if she was crying, she must still feel something. Anything would be better than that cool indifference.

He was torn. He knew he would risk a harsh, slicing rejection if he did what he wanted to do, yet it was tearing him apart to just stand here and watch her cry. A too-vivid image of how she must have cried six years ago seeped into his mind with the searing bite of acid; God, he was such a coward. He knew now he could never have faced her and told her that it had to end between them, because he could never have stood her tears.

He couldn't, he found, stand them now, and at last succumbed to the urgent need to hold her again and pulled her into his arms.

To his amazement, she didn't fight him. She seemed to sag against him, and he felt the little shuddering gulps as she tried to control her tears. He lifted a hand warily, tentatively, and brushed at the drops on her soft skin, drops that scalded him with guilt and soothed him with hope at the same time.

Looking down at the thick fringe of her wet, spiky lashes, Dev felt his heart begin to thud in fast, heavy beats. He'd never thought to even find her again, let alone touch her, or hold her, and that she was submitting so quietly to his embrace sent pulse after pulse of flaring heat and longing through him.

He slid his fingers slowly down the side of her face, feathering over her damp cheeks. Her skin was as soft, as silken as he remembered, and he knew he should back away before he did something that got him slapped. But he couldn't seem to do it. All he could do was lean forward and press his lips softly to the wetness, brushing at the remaining tears with his lips.

He heard her make a tiny little sound, and drew his head back. With a gentle finger he lifted her chin. His gaze met a pair of confused, shimmering blue eyes. He sensed her uncertainty as clearly as if she'd spoken it, and some deep, primal male instinct told him to move now, before she made up her mind that she still hated him.

He lowered his head slowly, more than a little uncertain himself. She didn't move away, although he gave her plenty of time to, and he had to clamp down on another surge of desperate hope. Then he felt her lips, soft, warm and impossibly willing beneath his, and he had no room for anything except the rushing response of his body.

He told himself to keep some fraction of space between them, or she would know that he was reacting to her as fiercely as ever, his body hardening with a speed that stunned him. It had been so long since he'd felt anything other than a dull numbness, yet she had burned through that frozen shell in seconds, dragging him back to life the way she had six years ago.

He found he couldn't bear even the small distance between them. He pulled her close, shivering with the intensity of his own reaction to holding her again. Only the great need for caution enabled him to gently, coaxingly caress her lips with his own, enabled him to stop himself from raiding the tempting honey that was so very close, so very sweet.

Dev wondered how he could still be standing when she made his knees so weak. It was still here, that instant fire, that danger that had lured him six years ago. He had to have more, to deepen the sweet but tentative kiss. But then she made a sound, a soft, whimpering sound that was painfully close to despair. Reluctantly, he wrenched his mouth from hers. He felt a shiver ripple through her.

"Meg...?"

"I..." She moved, an odd, jerky little motion. "I thought it would change...that it wouldn't be...like that anymore after..."

After what you did. The words echoed in his ears as clearly as if she'd spoken them. A chill swept him, sending the warmth before it like tiny riverbed pebbles pushed by the tumbling water.

"Meg," he began, but stopped, not knowing what to say.

She straightened then, pulling out of his arms, putting distance between them. She wiped at her eyes, then her damp cheeks.

"Megan," she insisted again. "Meggie doesn't exist anymore."

Dev winced inwardly as she again denied the precious memory that held so much pain, yet so much sweetness for him. But when he spoke, his voice was infinitely gentle. "Then who was that just now, kissing me?"

Her lips tightened, but her voice was even. "I wanted to know if I was still that little fool who was so blind she couldn't see the signs that were so obvious."

The wince was visible this time as Dev said, "So this was a test?"

"You could say that." Megan's mouth curved downward at one corner. "And I suppose you think I failed, don't you?

That all you have to do is kiss me, and I go up in flames just as I always did.''

Dev smothered the ripple of heat that shot through him at her words. "Did you?" he managed to ask.

"Go up in flames? Yes," she admitted honestly, despite the color staining her cheeks. "So I suppose I failed. But in a way I passed, as well. You see, there is a difference now. Meggie was a fool. All she knew was that she wanted you. I may still...want you, but I know that I can't afford you, Mr. Cross. I paid your kind of price once. I never will again. That's why Meggie doesn't exist anymore."

Dev wanted to cringe under the lash of her words, as if they were spoken with bitter sarcasm instead of her carefully neutral tone. After a moment, when he trusted his voice, he said, "I'm sorry for that. Meggie was a very special person." He saw something flicker in her eyes, some tiny spark of sadness. "You must miss her, sometimes," he said tentatively, and saw the momentary widening of her eyes that told him he'd hit home.

Then her gaze shifted to something beyond his shoulder, and he looked around to see Mason approaching with her father. When he turned back to Meg, she had put the dark glasses back on and was tidying her hair, tucking in the long, loose strands that had escaped. Dev remembered the short, shining, silken blond cap he'd known, and wondered how it would look now, long and down over her shoulders. If, he amended sadly, the perfect Megan ever let it down.

"—talk to them, but I can't promise you anything, Frank," Harlan was saying as they neared the car. "I have no control over their decisions."

"I know that," Mason was saying persuasively, "but you have a great deal of influence, Harlan. They'll listen to you."

"I said I'll speak to them," Harlan repeated, sounding a little irritated. "But I also said that I couldn't promise you anything."

"If you could just get them to back off—" Mason broke off suddenly, as if he only now realized how close they were to Dev and Megan.

They crossed the last few feet, and Harlan greeted Megan as he walked to the driver's door of the car. "All through, honey. Sorry to keep you so long."

"That's all right, Dad." There was no sign of emotional upheaval in her cool voice. "I had a chance to work on your speech a little."

Harlan smiled. "That's my girl, never satisfied. I told you it was fine yesterday."

"Is that for the Police Awards banquet?" Mason asked.

Harlan nodded. "One of my favorite ceremonies. I was happy to accept when the Chamber of Commerce called." He grinned. "It's easy when I have Megan to make a beautiful speech out of my chicken-scratch notes."

When Megan only shrugged, Harlan glanced at Dev, then back to her. "Were your ears burning? Did Dev tell you we were talking about you?"

Dev saw her stiffen. "No." Her voice was tight, almost brittle. "He didn't bother to mention that."

The reminder of other things he hadn't bothered to mention to her once was clear in her tone. Dev knew then that he was a long, long way from being forgiven. Odd, he thought vaguely, even throughout the pain he suffered, he had somehow thought that once she knew, she would be...more tolerant, perhaps. Then his mouth twisted ruefully. Meggie would have been; Megan was another story. She showed every sign of being as unyielding as granite. And you made her that way, he told himself acidly, so don't complain.

"We talked," he acknowledged at last.

"I see."

It wasn't a question or an accusation, but Dev winced as if it had been both. He phrased his answer carefully, aware of Harlan Spencer just a car-width away.

"We talked about . . . how plans change. And people."

"Sometimes you have to change." Megan's voice was even, unreadable. "Especially when you realize you've made a big mistake."

He didn't think his expression changed, but he felt that knot in his stomach tighten another notch. It had spread from his chest to his stomach the night of the party, and seemed to have dug in and settled to stay.

"No matter how big a mistake you make," he said, a little roughly, "there's always someone who's made a much worse, much bigger one."

He could feel her eyes on him, even though they were obscured now by the smoky lenses of her sunglasses.

"I think," she said after a moment, "that once you get to a certain point, the mistakes don't get any bigger. They just hurt more."

"Or hurt more people," he murmured, half under his breath, not even sure if he'd meant her to hear it. But she had; he could tell by the sudden tautness of her slender body, the slight thinning of her full mouth.

"But sometimes mistakes are worthwhile," she said, almost conversationally. "For instance, you might learn something about someone, something you never would have suspected."

He met her eyes then, sure of it despite the sunglasses, and without flinching he said, in a tone of the utmost resignation, "You mean that he's a coward? Yes. You might. And he might even learn it himself."

She drew back a fraction, as if surprised.

"If you two are through with this profound discussion," Harlan called, obviously puzzled by their cryptic conversation, "I think we'd better get going, Megan."

"Yes, Dad."

Her answer was quick, automatic, and just that quickly she was in the car and reaching for the ignition. Harlan quirked an eyebrow at her rudeness, but only called a goodbye for both of them as he got in, beside her this time, and closed the door.

Megan, safe behind the steering wheel, risked a look into the rearview mirror as she started the car. Dev was just standing there, watching the car pull away. Alone. Always alone. Even as close as they had once been, she had always felt that, yet even she had had no idea how utterly alone he'd really been.

She couldn't stop the feeling that welled up inside her then, that old combination of compassion, love and pure, aching longing. He'd always done that to her, always had that power over her.

Over Meggie, she corrected silently. He might have the same effect on Megan, but she had the strength, the weapons to fight it. True, that strength had wavered when she'd learned the truth about why he'd left her; she had been caught utterly off guard by the sheer cruelty of it.

It was just as well she'd been rendered speechless, she decided, carefully maneuvering the car through the construction site, because her first reaction had been a nearly overwhelming rush of compassion. She had had to fight the urge to call him back, to tell him she understood, to try and soothe away the old, remembered pain. And then she had heard Kevin's bright, childish laughter, and had come crashing back to reality.

Whatever his reasons had been, however brutal life had been to him, Devlin Cross was still the man who had never told her he was married, simple words that would have saved her so much anguish. And he was, she thought, her emotions an odd combination of hurt and satisfaction, apparently oblivious of the possibility that she had gotten pregnant, that he might have a child.

And that child, she knew, was the greatest weapon of all against her own weakness. She loved that little bundle of sandy-haired energy, and not for the world would she let him be hurt. Dev hadn't even acknowledged the possibility of his son's existence; she wasn't about to let him waltz in and lay some kind of claim to him now.

Not that he would, she added sourly. If he found out, he'd probably walk right out, like he had before. But she wasn't about to take any chances. Kevin was hers, and hers alone, and she intended to keep it that way.

"Megan?"

She forced a calm she didn't feel into her voice. She shot a glance at her father, who had the speech she'd been working on in his hands. "Yes, Dad?"

"Are you all right?"

"I'm fine."

"Are you sure? You looked a little . . . tense when I got back to the car."

"Just anxious to get going," Megan said brightly, hoping to divert him. "I've still got a lot of things to do for the party."

Harlan sighed. "You know, you didn't have to do this. I would have been just as happy to barbecue hamburgers at home with you and Kevin."

Megan managed a smile, glad he had taken the bait. "I know. But this is more politically correct."

Harlan grimaced. "Lord, I hate that phrase."

"Me, too. But believe me, Dad, if I hadn't planned this, somebody would have thrown you a surprise party, and you know you hate those even more."

"Now, that's a horrible thought."

"Besides, I don't mind. After all, it's not every day my father, the senator, turns fifty."

"Ouch," he said with an exaggerated mock grimace. "Don't remind me."

She slowed the car and then stopped as they approached the busy highway that ran by the construction site. She noticed her father looking at the rearview mirror. He seemed to be looking at the reflected image much longer than necessary, and something in his eyes when his gaze flicked back to Megan made her uneasy.

"Megan? Can just your father, not the senator, ask you something?"

"Of course." Her tone was natural, but her eyes had gone suddenly wary.

"Is there something going on between you and Dev Cross?"

She shifted her gaze forward, staring at the dashboard as if she'd never seen it before. "What on earth makes you say that?"

"Perhaps," her father said a little pointedly as he leaned forward so he could see her face, "the way you asked about him at the cocktail party the other night. And the electricity that was snapping between you two just now. Not to mention that rather odd conversation."

Megan slid her father a sideways glance. "I don't know what you mean."

"That's the same look you wore when you told me you didn't know how that frog got into the bathtub." Megan looked away again, coloring. "Okay, baby, I know it's none of my business. I just wondered because..."

Her chin came up. "Because?"

"I like him."

Megan didn't know what to say. When she'd dated as a teenager, her father had never said a word about any of the boys she'd seen, other than to tell her she'd better not have any ideas of getting serious until she was through college. Another piece of wise advice she'd ignored, she thought ruefully.

"I was thinking maybe we could invite him to the party."

Megan gaped at him. "Your birthday party?"

"Yes. Frank says he's pretty much alone up here, doesn't even go home to San Diego on the weekends."

"You want," Megan said carefully, "to invite Devlin Cross to your birthday party?"

Harlan shrugged. "I just thought it might be a nice thing to do. At least he'd know Frank, and me, and you. He's a good-looking young man, don't you think?"

Stunned, Megan didn't know what to say. Then something about her father's last words, and his very casualness struck her. Her eyes widened, and she stared him. "What are you up to, Dad? Are you...matchmaking or something? Is that why you want to invite him to the party?"

"Would that be so bad?"

If you only knew, Megan thought, paling. Her father looked at her in concern.

"Megan, it's just that I worry about you so. You work so hard, you never take any time for yourself. You give it all to me and Kevin. When was the last time you had a date?"

"I went to the deFirenzis' Halloween party."

He snorted. "With Leonard Wilson. You call an evening with my campaign manager a date? He's older than I am. Give someone your own age—like Dev—a chance."

Megan smothered an ironic groan. A chance. He wanted her to give Dev a chance. God, if he only knew that she'd given him so much more than that....

She took her foot off the brake, but replaced it when her father touched her shoulder. "I love you, Megan. I know you've been through hell, but please don't freeze the world out forever. For your sake. And Kevin's."

"I love you, too, Dad. So does your grandson. We'll be fine."

She knew he meant well, and she couldn't blame him when he didn't know. She'd made sure of that, that her powerful father had never known the identity of Kevin's father. It was the one thing she'd managed to accomplish in that devastating time. She hadn't let her father use his position to avenge her stupid mistake. Normally he would never do such a thing, but when it came down to the man who had left his beloved daughter a shattered shell, Megan knew that her father was hardly rational. If he ever found out Dev was the one . . .

She shuddered at the thought, then went still with shock when she realized it was now more at the idea of her father hating Dev than anything else. It was one thing for *her* to hate him for what he'd done, but somehow it didn't seem right for her father to think so horribly of him, not after all Dev had already been through.

And Kevin? The thought came to her suddenly, heart-stoppingly. She had managed to keep from thinking too much about the inevitable time when her son would ask about his father. But he would; she knew that. And when he did, what would she tell him?

There had been a time when she'd dreaded the possibility that her son might someday hate her for bringing him into the world without a father. Now she found herself worrying that when he was old enough to understand, he might hate her for never telling Dev about him. Especially if what Dev said was true, that he had looked for her. Or at least for the nonexistent Meg Scott.

But she, on the other hand, had always known where Dev was. Had he ever wondered why she hadn't tried to contact him? Or had he merely been grateful that she hadn't been around to remind him of what he'd done?

Meg smothered the shiver that swept her, knowing her father was very observant. She didn't know what she thought anymore, didn't know what she felt. Her emotions were in chaos, creating a near-unbearable pressure inside her. She wanted to run, as she had once before. Except this time she was already home and had nowhere to run to.

And this time she had someone else to think about, a gleeful little boy who reminded her so much of his father, in the way he held his head, the way his hair—a shade midway between her honey blond and Dev's sandy brown—had one stubborn lock that kicked forward over his brow, in the already determined strength of his jaw and the promise of the same lean, wiry strength in his small body. A little boy she loved with all her heart.

A little boy who might someday hate her because, thanks to his mother, his father didn't know he existed. That thought gave rise to an inner ache so strong it frightened her, but not nearly as much as the shocking realization that part of her pain was at the idea that, if he ever found out, Dev might hate her for the same reason.

Four

If only she'd gotten more sleep, Megan thought, she'd have been quick enough to think of a way to avoid this. But she'd been groggy from a long, restless night filled with unwanted dreams and images, and had gotten up early to take Kevin to his swimming lesson. When her father had asked her to go by the Gold Coast site and pick up some artist's renderings of the project for him to take back to his Sacramento office next week, she had only been able to stare blankly at him.

"You'll have time, won't you?" he'd asked, misinterpreting her lack of response. "Kevin's swimming session isn't over for a couple of hours, the speech is perfect as it is, you don't need to work on it anymore. And I'll take Martin to the airport on my way to the air quality meeting in L.A."

She gave him a vague smile. A lot of elected officials would have designated one of their aides to handle a personal chore such as taking a friend to the airport, but not

Harlan Spencer. "The taxpayer," he'd often said, "gets the short end often enough, without my using their money to shuttle my friends around." He "walked his talk," as the saying in the political arena went. He worked long and hard and honestly, and Megan loved and respected him for it. As she had once loved and respected another man who worked long and hard and honestly, naively assuming that honesty carried over into his personal life as well.

And the little fool she'd been then would have believed anything, she told herself acidly, hoping to chivy herself out of the painful longing that had settled on her deep in the night when dreams of Dev had overtaken her.

"Megan? Are you still with me?"

"Of course, Dad," she said automatically.

"Good. I told Frank you'd be by this morning. It will only take a moment. Then you take the rest of the day off." A speculative glint came into her father's eyes. "Maybe you'll see Dev Cross there."

Megan paled a little; her father didn't seem willing to drop this idea he'd latched on to. "It wouldn't matter," she said a little shortly. "I hardly know the man." And that, she added in silent emphasis, is the exact truth.

"I know," Harlan said, the look in his eyes changing to one of warm, parental concern. "But at least you didn't treat him with that royal disdain you turn on virtually every other man you meet."

"I do not!"

"Megan, Megan. It's become so automatic you don't even realize it. Anytime a man starts to get the least bit close to you, you freeze up and drive him away."

"Perhaps I like it that way," she returned stiffly.

"I know you do. My sweet, loving little hellion has turned into an aloof princess with ice in her eyes."

Megan's eyes widened. "I thought you were happy with me this way."

"I am. You're beautiful, regal, the perfect hostess, a world-class organizer and smart enough to puncture some of the pompous windbags I have to deal with in such a clever way that they don't even realize what's been done to them. Everything I ever hoped you would be."

Gently he reached out and took her hand, clasping it between his. "But, to my surprise, sometimes I find that I desperately miss that hair-raising little scamp who was looking for excitement around every corner and expected every day to be the day that brought it."

Incredibly touched, Megan blinked rapidly as she tightened her fingers around her father's. "Sometimes," she whispered, "I miss her, too."

"Then try to find her again, baby. Somehow I don't think you'll ever be a whole person until you do."

Those words echoed in her mind as she drove her low-slung, immaculate Corvette carefully over the rough, dirt track at the construction site. The car had been a gift from her father after his reelection to the Senate last year, presented to her with a kiss and a half-serious quip about buying American to keep his constituents happy. She'd thought the selection odd at the time; the racy little yellow sports car hardly fit the poised, polished woman she'd worked so hard to become. Now she wondered if he hadn't been, in some subtle way, telling her then what he'd finally told her today.

"I'm sorry, Daddy," she whispered as she parked, "but I've lost that girl forever."

She knew it was true; nothing ever stirred her to the heights and depths of emotion she'd felt then; at least, nothing had until that night she'd turned around and seen Dev standing there.

Dev.

She stopped in the midst of maneuvering out of the car, staring at the battered black Jeep that sat parked beside Frank Mason's Mercedes. He was here, then.

Of course he was, she thought sourly. Isn't that how your luck has been running? Then her brow creased as something else occurred to her: if Cross Consulting was doing so well, why hadn't he bought a new car? That one had to be at least ten years old now, with who knew how many rough, torturous miles on it; he'd told her of all the distant, remote places he'd taken it on jobs. And she knew it was the same Jeep, she'd ridden in it a few times, she remembered the row of old university parking stickers—

Oh, admit it, she demanded of herself silently, you had every inch of that thing memorized. You could have picked it out in a crowd of black Jeeps, just like you could pick him out of a crowd of lean, six-foot males in an instant.

Her gaze flicked from the downtrodden utility vehicle to the long, white trailer, festooned with temporary power lines running in from the main lines back on the highway. Maybe he wasn't inside. Maybe, she thought with rising hope, he and Frank were out on the site somewhere. Maybe—

Stop it! She straightened her spine as she snapped the order to herself. On top of all the other nights to be laid at his door, he cost you last night's sleep. You're not going to let him ruin this unexpected day off. Go in, get the drawings and get out. Simple.

Driven by that determination, she walked steadily over to the trailer. The door was ajar, and the sound of a raised voice stopped her at the bottom of the steps.

"Damn it, Dev, that kind of delay is going to cost me a bundle!"

Dev's voice came then, low and calm. "I know. But it's the only way to do it safely."

"It can't be!"

Dev's voice again, sympathetic but firm. "Sorry, Frank. But you saw the reports on those last core samples. The density and stability just aren't there. That stretch of decomposed granite runs out right here," he said, over the sound of paper rustling, "and you're into sandy loam. That whole area is going to have to be compacted."

"That could take weeks!"

Dev said something she couldn't hear, then the rustling of papers came again. When he spoke again, his voice still calm but unwavering, the words were clear.

"Maybe not. If you excavate this area first, bring in the water and other material to mix with it and do the compacting while you're excavating another section over here... And it looks like you might have enough adobe-type clay from up near the highway, which would save you having to truck it in—"

"You don't get it, do you—every damned day will cost me a small fortune!"

Dev sounded faintly puzzled. "You must have expected this. The whole south coast is made up of this kind of soil."

"But I didn't expect this much. This is practically the whole damn project! And I suppose you're going to tell me it's going to require ninety-eight percent compaction?"

"I'm not," Dev answered mildly. "The state is."

Mason swore, low and harsh, and Megan barely had time to back out of the way when she heard his heavy, angry footsteps headed toward the door. The big man barely smiled at her as he swept past.

"Drawings are on the desk," he said shortly, and was gone.

Megan was surprised. Despite his anger, Frank Mason was wise enough not to offend her father, which meant he couldn't offend her. And while she might think him pushy and overbearing, the man had always been courteous to her. But then, she'd never seen him at work before, and from the sound of things—thanks to Dev's findings—it wasn't going well.

Unwillingly she found herself admiring the way he'd stood up to the gruff, autocratic man. He'd stayed cool, unruffled, and quietly stuck to his guns. But then, she'd never questioned his dedication to his work.

Steeling herself, she walked up the steps. She had dressed more appropriately this time. While her shirt was a pale blue silk and her slacks a fine linen, on her feet were rubber-soled espadrilles, and she made no sound as she walked up the short metal stairway. The door was still open; surprisingly Frank hadn't slammed it in his angry exit. She came to a halt on the top step, trying to gather her courage before Dev looked up and noticed her.

He was sitting on a drafting stool, his elbows propped on the surface of the high table in the corner of the room. The sleeves of his blue chambray shirt were rolled midway up his forearms, exposing the cords of muscle that melded with the strong tendons of his hands. His face was buried in those hands, and weariness cried out from every line of his lean, drooping body. His thick hair was tousled, and for an instant Megan flashed back to that day when he'd stood outside the café, fighting that inner battle.

She knew now that he'd been fighting to stay away from her, a realization that stung. But she knew as well that he'd been in agony. She might not be certain of anything else, but she knew that. She'd known it then as she knew it now, but now she resented the instinctive tug of pain she felt inside. She didn't want to feel compassion for him.

She must have made some small sound in her battle to suppress that unwanted emotion, because he looked up. The exhaustion that had been so evident was replaced with a sudden tautness, and he stared at her, hazel eyes alight with a look that sent a tiny shiver racing down her spine.

"Meg," he breathed.

"Megan," she corrected automatically, fighting that little frisson of sensation. She almost wished she hadn't when that light vanished from his eyes.

"Excuse me," he said formally. "I keep forgetting."

Strain made her words a little sharp. "You always had a very selective memory."

He paled, and an anguish as deep as any she'd seen before flashed in his eyes. He swayed a little on the chair, and for a moment she thought he was going to topple over. Then he steadied himself, just as she was realizing in astonishment that she had been about to go to him, to hold him and tell him she hadn't meant it.

"It's all right," he said wearily. "I understand. I was a fool for thinking you might..." He looked away, staring down at the charts before him on the table. "You have every right to hate me."

To her amazement, Megan found herself denying the words she'd spoken to herself so often. She couldn't say them somehow, here, to his face, knowing what he'd been through.

"No." It was barely audible, but it brought Dev's head up sharply. "I... tried. I wanted to hate you. But I couldn't. I didn't have the strength. All I could do was... hurt."

"Because I'd drained all your strength," Dev said bitterly. "I used it to keep myself going."

"No." The denial came again, nearly as soft as the first. "It made me stronger, knowing you... needed me. At least... who I was, then."

"God, Meggie..."

Her body went suddenly taut. She'd heard those words, that tone, before, and the memory of when and where came flooding back, bringing her anger roaring back to life. This was the man who'd left her to wake up alone on a morning when no woman should be alone. This was the man who had lacked the courage to say the simple words that would have saved her untold pain.

"I know," he said, as if he'd sensed the change in her. "That's no excuse, Meggie—Megan. Not for what I did to you." He looked away again, as if he expected to see assent in her eyes and couldn't bear it. "I was a selfish bastard. I used you, lied to you, hurt you unforgivably. I fed on your youth and energy and spirit like a leech, and then turned on you in the most horrible way, at the most horrible time. I destroyed that youth, and your trust, and now I know I did something even worse. I destroyed your dreams."

Megan was staring at him now, wide-eyed. He was saying everything she'd told herself, all the things she'd tried to believe about him in the desperate days after he'd left her, in the days when she was trying so hard to put her life back together, trying to cope with the knowledge that she never could. She'd believed all the ugly words then, or told herself she did, so why did it sound so utterly appalling now? Why did it seem so very excessive coming from him, in that cold, implacable tone of self-contempt?

"Dev," she whispered, unable to stop the tiny sound's escape.

He cringed as if the sound of his name from her was some unbearable pain. When he spoke again, his voice was hoarse, barely a whisper.

"And you know the real hell of it?" His head came up, and a pair of tortured hazel eyes met her stunned blue gaze. "I still love you. I loved you then, and I still—"

With a sharp, convulsive movement he turned away from her, lowering his head. She saw him blink rapidly, then squeeze his eyes shut tightly.

It was too much. With a smothered little cry she whirled and ran, nearly falling as she tried to go down the trailer steps in a rush.

Damn him, she thought as she jammed her foot down on the accelerator of the Corvette. Damn him for saying it now, when he never had in all the time they'd been together. Damn him for saying it when it was too late to salvage anything of what had been between them. Damn him for having that uncanny power to demolish her pride and make her want to comfort, to console him, when *he'd* been the one to cause so much pain, so much devastation. Damn him for making her pulse race at the sight of him. And damn him most of all for still being able to make her heart leap, in spite of everything, at the thought that he loved her.

"Damn him!"

It burst from her on a sob of fury as she yanked the steering wheel around. The tires squealed as she pulled out onto the pavement of Coast Highway and headed back into town. After a moment she caught herself and eased off the accelerator. The local police were diligent about slowing down the drivers who took the mostly empty stretch outside of Aliso Beach at high speed. Devlin Cross had already cost her her heart, her dreams, and most of her joy in life; she'd be damned if she'd let him cost her a speeding ticket.

Besides, she had someone else to think about. She wasn't about to get herself killed driving like the emotional maniac she seemed to have turned into lately, and leave Kevin without a mother as well as without a father. She took a deep breath, and tried to push that father out of her mind.

Dev wanted to go and shut the door, wanted to lock it so that no one could walk in on him until he was back in control, but he didn't trust his shaky legs to carry him even the dozen or so feet across the narrow interior of the trailer.

He couldn't believe he'd done it. He'd sworn he would be as coolly formal as she was the next time he saw her, that he would let the past die as she so obviously wanted it to. But he'd been no more successful at that than he had been at staying away from her six years ago, and he began to wonder if he had any backbone at all.

He stifled a sigh, letting his head drop back into his hands. His weary mind recoiled from the intensity of the emotions just roused, trying feebly to quash the hope that had flickered within him when she'd said she didn't hate him. The hope that had flared hotly to life in that frozen moment when she had whispered his name.

It was bad enough that he'd told her he loved her, that he hadn't been able to keep that useless knowledge locked inside. But to take that one breathless moment and somehow imagine that there had been a softening in her, to imagine that she had sounded almost as she had all those years ago, was foolishness beyond belief. And to continue with that fanciful thinking would cost him dearly, out of an account that was already far overdrawn.

He lifted his head, rubbing at his eyes with the heels of his hands, wishing he could remember what it felt like to not be tired. It seemed years since he'd felt truly rested. His mouth twisted sourly. Maybe it *had* been years.

He leaned back on the stool, stretching, trying to beat some life back into weary muscles. As he moved, his gaze came to rest on the large blue folder that sat on the desk next to the table.

The drawings. That was why she'd come, he realized suddenly. He hadn't even thought about it when he'd looked up to see her in the doorway, he'd merely accepted her presence as if his thoughts of her had conjured her up.

He sat for a long time, staring at the folder with her father's name scrawled across it in Frank Mason's conspicuous hand. He told himself once more that he was being a fool, that there had been no momentary change in Megan Spencer. There had not been a fleeting, flashing glimpse of Meggie in that cool, blond facade. There had been, at most, a brief flicker of pity, the very thing he'd put them both through hell to avoid. And it had been rapidly followed by anger, her own anger at herself for feeling any leniency at all toward him.

Yes, he was a fool, he thought as he reached over and picked up the folder, but it certainly wasn't the first time, and he ruefully doubted that it would be the last.

Megan stopped her restless pacing when the phone rang. Let the machine get it, she thought. She certainly didn't feel like talking to anyone right now. She reached the mantel of the library's fireplace and turned to start back in her crossing and recrossing of the room. Then she stopped abruptly.

No, she didn't want to talk to anyone, she thought in disgust; she'd much rather go back and forth across this room like a rat trapped in a cage. She stalked over to the phone on her father's desk and grabbed the receiver just as the answering machine came on. She turned it off and tried to keep the anger at herself out of her voice. "Hello."

"Miss Spencer? This is Ray down at the gate."

She relaxed a little. "Yes, Ray. What is it?"

"There's a kid here with something to deliver to the senator. Some drawings, from Mr. Mason. He says you're expecting them."

She groaned inwardly; how could she have forgotten the reason she'd gone out there in the first place? Never mind, she told herself, she knew how. And now Frank had had to send one of his workers out with them. He knows you were there to get them, she muttered to herself; he probably thinks you're a fumbling idiot now.

"Yes, Ray," she said into the phone, "it's all right."

"Okay, Miss Spencer. I'll send him on up."

At least it wasn't Frank, she thought as she waited for the ringing of the doorbell. She wouldn't be faced with trying to explain why she'd walked out and left the very thing she'd come for.

By the time the bell chimed, she had herself reasonably under control. Prepared with a polite "thank you" on her lips, she pulled open the heavy, carved oak front door.

"You?"

It was a gasp; too late she remembered that Ray, a crusty, retired police officer who was nearing seventy, had a habit of referring to anyone under forty as a kid.

His expression giving nothing away, Dev held out the blue folder. "Been a while since anyone called me kid."

"I . . . Thank you," she said. "I must have—"

She broke off suddenly, seeing the ridiculousness of explaining to him why she'd forgotten the drawings.

"Yes," he said as if she'd said the words. "I know. You were upset. I'm sorry."

Embarrassment flooded her, and she couldn't help the sharpness that crept into her tone. "You're sorry I was upset?"

He didn't wince, he didn't seem to react at all, but in his voice was a sharp undertone that echoed the self-contempt that had disturbed her so before. "No. I'm sorry that *I* upset you. Small difference, but true. I had no right to say what I said."

Her breath caught. "You mean saying that you . . ."

"Love you," he said, as flatly as if he were indeed that delivery boy she'd been expecting. "You didn't want to hear it, but I had to tell you." The undertone deepened, became harsher. "I seem to have a knack for doing what I need at your expense."

His expression changed at last, and for a moment it was as if she'd stepped back in time. He looked as haunted, as spent as he had looked on those long-ago days in the café. Instinctively she lifted a hand to touch him.

"Oh, Dev, I—"

"Don't!" He jerked away, sucking in a swift, harsh breath. "Don't touch me. Don't sound like that."

Stunned, and furious with herself for the weakness he seemed to cause in her resolve, Megan yanked her hand back. Then, perversely, he grabbed it, the folder of drawings falling unnoticed to the porch.

"Please, don't," he whispered harshly, and when his eyes met hers, all the torture of the last five years was in them. "When your voice goes soft like that, when you touch me, you make me think there's hope, and I know there isn't."

She could have sworn that in those tortured hazel eyes was an entreaty, as if he were begging her to prove him wrong. Megan stared at him, her emotions in an uproar. That insidious softness, that tenderness she couldn't seem to control around him, warred with the acid-etched memory of what he'd done, and the anger at herself she'd never quite been able to let go of, anger that she had been such a fool. Neither seemed able to win, and as a result she stood immobilized, unable to move or stop the confusion she knew was showing on her face. She lowered her gaze to keep him from seeing it.

Pulling her hand free, Megan backed up a step, reaching blindly for the handle of the door, the need to flee this pained confusion uppermost in her mind. She bumped the heavy oak panel, and it swung away from her, baring several of the black and white marble squares of the entry. She hated that floor, she thought inanely. Made her feel like a pawn on a chessboard.

She saw Dev bend to pick up the folder he'd dropped. He straightened up and held it out to her once more.

"You don't have to run, Megan. I'll leave."

She took the drawings with a hand that was none too steady. For an instant their fingers brushed, and Megan felt a little burst of heat rippling out from the contact. Dev looked at her with an expression of sad resignation.

"It's still there, isn't it?" he whispered. "At least *that* isn't gone."

Something in his wistful tone tugged at a heart that had borne too much already this morning. "Maybe," she said rather stiffly, "because that was all there was to begin with."

He drew back, his mouth tightening as pain flashed once more in his eyes. "You can't believe that."

"Oh?"

"No! You know it was more, that I..."

His voice trailed off and his eyes were full of such anguish that Megan felt that old tenderness welling up inside her. She fought it back.

"I don't know how you do this to me," she ground out, "but I'm not going to let you, not this time."

Dev let out a long, weary breath. "You didn't *let* me before, Meg. I took advantage of your innocence. I think I knew that it would never occur to you that I was married. And I used that. I needed what you gave me so badly, I needed you to be the one bright spot in my life, separate from all the rest, to be the one person who didn't look at me like I was someone to feel sorry for."

Megan paled, her anger fading again. Could she even begin to realize what it had been like for him? She tried to imagine it, the enormity of the helplessness he must have felt, caught by circumstances beyond his control, his wife gone from him for years in all except body, himself neither married nor free. A long moment of silence spun out, broken only by the sound of a car coming up the hill.

"You see?" he said then, softly. "Even now, you have that look, that damn look of pity on your face. Like everybody else did. 'Poor Dev,' they all said. Wonder how he stands it. Wonder how long it'll be before he falls apart. Too bad, his life ruined, and so young—"

His voice had turned bitter with remembrance, and he suddenly stopped the flow of words as if he realized what he sounded like. When he spoke again, the sourness was gone, but the sadness remained. "I know now I was right about that, at least. I knew I couldn't take that look of pity from you. Anybody else, but not you."

"Dev, I . . ."

Her voice faded. She didn't know what to say. And then, as she saw something out of the corner of her eye, panic struck her, as solid and real as the station wagon that was coming up the street. God, she should have realized, should have paid attention to the time.

But it was too late now. Mrs. Moreland was already pulling into the driveway, waving as she came to a stop at the top of the curved drive, near the front door. Megan saw Dev turn to look. The passenger door of the wagon popped open. Megan quickly started down the steps, not sure of her own intentions, only hoping that she could somehow avoid disaster. And then it was upon her.

"Mommy, Mommy!" Kevin's words were high, eager and undeniably directed at her as the boy scrambled out of the car and ran toward her, barely sparing a glance at the stranger who stood beside her. "I did good today, Carla said so! She said I could prob'ly swim with the Minnows soon! I'm tired of bein' a Tadpole."

Tensely, Megan bent to hug her excited son. "Good for you, honey. Go change out of your wet suit now, okay? Then you can tell me all about it."

Megan patted him encouragingly, and he scampered inside without a backward glance. The station wagon pulled around the corner toward the garage, out of sight. Megan straightened up. She fiddled with a bent corner of the folder that held the drawings. And at last, with the greatest effort she'd made at anything since Kevin's birth, she raised her head to look at Dev's stunned, pale face.

Five

"He's not yours, you know."

Dev's stunned gaze jerked back to her from the door the small, thin child had left open behind him. Megan could easily see what he was feeling. His defenses had been shattered by shock. She tried again, doing her best to hide her panic.

"Don't bother to count it up," she said sharply, desperation putting an edge in her voice, "*if* you can even remember. Kevin is months too young to be yours."

She thought she could get away with it. Kevin had come weeks early, after a difficult first pregnancy, and had not quite caught up yet in size. For once she was grateful that he looked younger than his five-plus years. She was praying Dev would be convinced. She watched him carefully, watched the shock fade to be replaced by an expression she didn't understand until he spoke at last.

"I... It didn't...take you long, did it?" he said hoarsely.

Her brow furrowed. "Take me long . . . ?"

"To find somebody else."

Megan gasped. She should be glad he'd bought her lie, she told herself, but all she could seem to feel was a sharp, knifing pain as she made sense out of that look on his face. He was reeling under the impact of what she hadn't thought of in her hasty attempt to divert him from his inevitable assumption—that if Kevin wasn't his, she must have gone almost immediately to another man.

Instinctively a protest rose to her lips. She smothered it with an effort. He'd believed her—that was all that mattered. Besides, he has no right to be upset, she told herself firmly. *He'd* left *her,* not the other way around. And even if she could accept his reasons for that, she would never forgive him for not telling her he was married before she'd given him her heart, her body and her very soul.

And for not coming back to her when he could have. She'd stayed put in San Diego for six weeks, even when her every instinct was to run for home, yet he'd never tried to contact her, to find out if there had been any . . . aftereffects of that single, passionate night. He'd made a clean break, apparently not caring what else he might have left behind.

"I was on the rebound," she said shortly. "What did you expect?"

She was a horrible liar, she knew that, but for Kevin's sake, she would learn. She would have to, because this was a lie she could feel growing even now. For the moment, Dev's shock had gotten her through, but she knew this wasn't the end. Unless, she thought grimly, she'd managed to hurt him so badly in turn that he left her—and her son— alone.

Hurt wasn't the word for what Dev was feeling as he drove away. He knew he was in pain, yet an odd numbness had spread through him, as if he were at a distance somehow, watching himself suffer. He wondered if it was some odd function of his brain, a brain that knew perfectly well that he had no right to be hurt that she, in her own pain, pain that *he* had caused, had turned to someone else. A brain that knew he had no rights at all when it came to Megan Spencer. Or her son. The boy who could have been his.

But wasn't. He could see that, Dev thought. He'd have to be past five, and this boy couldn't be. This child was about the size of his nephew, who wouldn't be five for a couple of months yet. But he wasn't that much younger, which led Dev straight back to the stunning knowledge that Meg had gone straight from him to someone else.

What did you expect? he asked under his breath. He'd hurt her so badly, and she'd been so very young.... It was only natural that she had fallen into the arms of the first man to be kind to her.

And into his bed.

The words spun in his head, setting up an echoing spin of that knot that had settled in the pit of his stomach. The thought of Meggie giving herself to another man, of some other man taking again and again the sweetness he had tasted first, made him nearly drive off the road.

At least he took her *in* a bed, he told himself acidly. Not on the floor, half-drunk and in a frenzy. He yanked the wheel around, the squeal of the tires a fitting counterpoint to his mood. He pulled out past the security gate and onto the main road. As his speed picked up, so did the pace of his whirling thoughts.

Did she love him, this man she'd borne a son to? She'd said she'd been on the rebound, but that didn't mean she hadn't come to love the man who—unlike himself—had been there for her when she'd needed him. And where was he now? She wore no ring. She was living in her father's house and using her father's name, she who had been so determined not to garner any favors because of that name.

Where the hell was her son's father? Why wasn't he here, taking care of them? What kind of man would walk away from a woman like Megan, and their son?

A man like you, his conscience put in mercilessly.

A sudden shudder of realization swept him. His teeth clenched against the sudden tightening of that knot in his belly. A blaring honk warned him he was out of control, and he pulled shakenly to the side of the road, his foot slipping off the clutch and stalling the Jeep.

My God, he thought. No wonder Meg hates you. He slumped forward, resting his forehead against hands that were shaking even though clasped around the steering wheel. He'd never thought of it. It had simply never occurred to him that the one time he'd made love to her—that first time for her, a time that should have been so special—could have left her pregnant.

He supposed it was a sign of the pressure he'd been under then that he'd never thought of it. Or perhaps, he acknowledged grimly, he hadn't let himself think of it. The idea of a child, his and Meg's child, was far too tempting, even now. Back then it would have overwhelmed him. It would have been the last straw, his breaking point, and perhaps his weary mind had known it.

But Meg hadn't known it. All she had known was that he had left her alone after she'd given him the precious gift of herself. And then she had found out, through the cold harshness of an impersonal phone call, why he'd left her. At least, it was the why she had carried in her heart for nearly six years. He owed her, it seemed, one more apology.

With a promise to his battered emotions that this was the last time, that after this there would be nothing left but to walk away, to leave it behind, he restarted the Jeep and pulled back onto the road, exceeding a sweeping U-turn.

*	*	*

Megan wasn't sure how she knew, since she had no reason to expect him back so soon, but the moment Mrs. Moreland came upstairs to tell her she had a visitor, she knew who it was. He'd forgotten something, Mrs. Moreland said. Megan couldn't imagine what was left to say. She took a moment to be certain her voice would be steady, then called out through the closed bedroom door that she would be down in a moment.

She sat up on her bed, the sound of her movement over the satin comforter the only sound in the dimness of the room. She had pulled down the shades to shut out the sun, as if the lack of light would help her hide from her tangled emotions. It hadn't worked.

Even Kevin had sensed something, stopping in the midst of his chatter about his successful swimming lesson to ask what was wrong. She had pleaded a headache, and hated the lie even more at the concern that furrowed his young face. And nearly cried at his solemn instructions for her to take an aspirin and go lie down like Grandpa did when he got "a ache in his head."

Minus the aspirin and plus letting her hair down out of its usual perfection, she had done as she'd been told by her five-year-old physician, but there was no simple solution to the emotional chaos she'd been cast into with the return of Devlin Cross. Of all the possible explanations for his behavior, the truth was one she'd never, ever expected.

She'd never been able to reconcile his behavior with her perception of him, and therefore had come to the only conclusion possible to her: since what he'd done was an immutable fact, it had to be her perception that was wrong. She'd carried a deep and festering self-contempt for her own blindness, her own foolishness, for so long that she no longer knew if she could ever let go of it. Even the exterior of the perfect, poised, polished woman was only a hard-won facade, so that no one would discover the little fool who hid behind it.

Yet now the perception that she'd held for so long was shaken. The man she'd tried to convince herself was a cold, calculating user had in fact been a man caught in an impossible situation, truly as torn as she had first thought him. Yet did that excuse what he'd done? Did that make up for the pain she'd gone through? For the humiliation of having to face her father and tell him just how right he'd been, just what a naive little fool she was? For the horrible, rending loneliness of having to fight her way through a pregnancy that seemed to want to end itself time and again, as if her baby had been aware of the turmoil his mother was in, and not at all certain of his welcome into this world?

Slowly she walked into her bathroom. One look in the mirror told her she wasn't going to be able to disguise all of the ravages of her emotional state. She did her best with some concealer on the bruised looking circles beneath her eyes, and some color on her cheeks, then ran a brush through her tousled hair. Automatically she reached up to twist the blond mass into a tight, neat coil at the back of her neck.

When it was secure, she took a deep breath and she studied herself in the mirror. And then, with more care and as much artifice, she applied the practiced facade once more and became the smooth, polished senator's daughter. And prayed that the image would hold up before the one man who had the power to shatter it. She left the room, wondering with trepidation what Dev had come back for.

When she got downstairs, the foyer was empty. She crossed to the drawing room, thinking Mrs. Moreland had shown him to a chair, but it, too, was empty. Kevin's trill of cheerful laughter from the family room made her instinctively smile, but when the laugh was followed by a low, unmistakably male voice, Megan felt a chill sweep through her. She barely kept herself from running toward the sounds.

She came to an abrupt halt in the doorway of the family room, her heart hammering as it seemed to rise and catch in her throat. She had expected the mess spread out over the oaken coffee table. Kevin had been working on the simple, children's model of the Blackbird stealth plane for over a week now, with a determination and patience that had amazed her. What she hadn't expected was Dev, sitting cross-legged on the floor beside the boy, watching intently.

Megan stood as if paralyzed, staring at father and son. Kevin was holding one wing of the airplane up to the fuselage—unfortunately upside down.

"You know," Dev said thoughtfully, not a trace of a smile on his face, "I think you may have had it right the first time."

The boy glanced at Dev a little shyly, then turned the wing back the right way. "You mean, this way?"

Dev nodded, then pointed at the box the model had come in. "See, you were right."

"It does look like the picture now, doesn't it?" Kevin said eagerly, and reached for the glue.

"Want me to hold it so you can concentrate on the tricky stuff? I can see how careful you are about not getting too much glue on it."

"Grandpa said I had to be real careful," Kevin agreed, accepting Dev's help without a protest, which was amazing in itself, Megan thought, considering the child's determination to do this himself. Dev had been more than tactful, he had been as considerate of the boy's feelings as . . . a father.

Megan had to back out of the room, afraid that she was going to lose her battle to control the moisture that was suddenly brimming behind her eyelids. A fierce emotion, so strong and deep that she didn't know if it was pain or pleasure, clawed at something deep inside her.

Then she heard Kevin laugh again, and panic returned in a flood. *Was* Dev acting like a father? Had he guessed, somehow, that she had lied? Had he seen the subtle resemblances that were so clear to her? Was that why he'd come back? Alarm propelled her back into the room.

"Mom, look!" Kevin cried as he heard her rapid steps. "It really looks like the Blackbird now!"

"I see that, Kevin," she said, her voice taut. "Why don't you keep working on it while Mr. Cross and I go talk in the drawing room?"

Kevin's brow furrowed at her tone. Dev rose slowly to his feet. It was clear by his expression that he, too, had noticed her anxiety. He watched her face, as if searching for something.

"Do you still have your headache, Mom?" Kevin asked.

She tried to soften the edge in her voice for her son. "I'm fine, honey." The softer tone slipped a little as she gestured toward the door. "If you would, Mr. Cross?"

Dev's gaze flicked to Kevin, then back to Megan. He didn't move, but she sensed his recoil as realization chilled his eyes. She saw him tense, bracing as if expecting a blow...or perhaps to shake off one already received. He had guessed, she knew, that she wanted him away from her son. She could only imagine what he was thinking her reasons were, and hope that he wasn't anywhere near the truth.

Dev moved past her somewhat stiffly as, with impeccable and pointed politeness, she waited in the doorway for him.

"Thanks for helpin' me, Dev."

Dev stopped dead at the boy's words and glanced back over his shoulder.

"You're welcome," he said softly, and Megan knew the moment he spoke that she'd been right about the tension in him; it rang beneath the gentle words.

When they reached the drawing room, where they had first seen each other again amidst a throng of people, Megan stopped, and Dev turned to face her. His tension and her agitation seemed to feed on each other, and the silence grew strained.

"He's a nice kid," Dev said at last.

"Yes." It was short, clipped, and she hastened to divert him. "What do you want?"

Megan saw him glance back toward the family room, and her heart began to hammer once more. Had he guessed?

"I wish..." he began slowly, still looking toward the room where even now they could hear Kevin carrying on a cheerful conversation with Mrs. Moreland.

"Don't," Megan snapped, her control slipping. Dev's gaze shot back to her. "What do you want?" she repeated.

Pain glinted in the hazel eyes, then disappeared, as if he had closed himself off to her. "For starters," he said tightly, "where's his father?"

Megan tried not to let her gasp of relief escape. It was a moment before she was able to answer. "We're not together anymore. Kevin and I both use my name. Kevin never knew him."

The misleading truth came out smoothly enough; she'd had time now to plan this answer, all the while hoping she'd never have to face the question.

"Not," she added with emphasis, "that it's any of your business."

Dev winced slightly, just the barest change in expression, so swift Megan wasn't sure she'd seen it. She saw him take a deep breath, then let it out in a long, controlled exhalation.

"No," he said at last, "I suppose it's not. Nothing about you is, is it?"

Megan didn't answer, only pride forcing her to hold his gaze. It made her stomach churn; his eyes looked as hollow and haunted as they had six years ago.

"You know," he said slowly, "I really did try to find you."

"So you said. Funny, I was there. In my apartment. For six weeks after you walked out. Even though I hated the place, hated the memories—"

She broke off sharply when she heard her voice start to rise. She'd had no intention of letting him know how much he'd hurt her. She steadied herself, then went on with a cool shrug.

"Silly little fool that I was, I waited, hoping." Hoping you'd come back and explain how you could have done such a thing, she added silently. Hoping it was all a mistake, and you weren't really married. Hoping I wasn't really pregnant...

Dev shifted uncomfortably on his feet. "I mean afterward."

She felt a retort rising to her lips, but even in her anger the thought of blaming the woman who had died so young for the mess Megan had made of her own life filled her with shame. It wasn't the fault of a woman dead for years that you were such a fool, Megan told herself sternly. If anything, Dev's wife had been the innocent victim.

"I tried," Dev repeated, "but by then you were gone. At least, Meg Scott was gone. I guess you had already become Megan Spencer."

"I always was Megan Spencer. Meg Scott was just...a silly child, a phase I had to outgrow."

"Don't!" It broke from him as if against his will. "Don't say that. Meg was a sweet, innocent, beautiful person. Don't throw her away, just because I—"

Megan waited when he stopped, but he just shook his head as if in pain. Then he straightened, squaring his broad shoulders.

"I'm sorry. I didn't come back here to drag all that out again."

"Then why did you come back?"

He took a quick, deep breath. "To apologize."

"Again?"

"Not . . . about that. I've told you I never meant to hurt you. And I know you don't believe it. There's nothing I can do about that. I can't change the past."

"Then what?"

"I just . . . I only just realized . . ." He stopped, running a hand through the tousled thickness of his hair, a gesture so endearingly familiar Megan had to steel herself against the pang it caused. "God, what's the use. You won't believe this, either. It's absurd. I barely believe it myself."

"Believe what?"

Turning away from her, Dev walked to the large, small-paned window that looked out on the great circular driveway. His fingers curled as his hands clenched into fists. He jammed them into his pockets as if stopping himself from taking a swing at something.

Megan watched him, safe now since his back was turned, wondering why she was even listening to this man who had caused her so much pain. She was studying him so intently, trying not to notice the way the tug of his hands in his pockets had snugged his jeans to the taut curve of his buttocks, that when he began to speak again she nearly jumped.

His voice was low and rough, but even had it been normal, she would have known how hard this was for him. It was evident in every wiredrawn line of his body, every slow, painful pause as he dragged out the words.

"I was on the edge then, Meg—" He caught himself. "Megan. You knew that. You always knew that, didn't you? That something was wrong?"

"I knew."

Dev turned back to face her, fists still jammed into his pockets, his expression tight, as if he expected her to throw his words back in his face, but had to say them anyway.

"I don't think I realized how close I was to breaking, until I met you." He started to lower his eyes, then lifted his gaze back to meet hers, as if he was forcing himself to do it. "I didn't realize I was going over that edge until you pulled me back. I didn't realize that I was on the verge of losing it, of shattering into a million pieces. One more thing, one more ounce of pressure, and I . . ."

"Do you think I don't know that?" Megan said tightly. "Do you think I didn't sense something was crushing you?" She didn't want to feel this, didn't want to be reminded of his pain; it made her want to comfort him, even now, and that was territory far too dangerous for her to venture into. "Look, I'm sorry for what happened to your wife. No one deserves to die so young, especially like that. And I'm sorry—"

"No!"

He crossed the room in one long stride, grabbing her shoulders as he repeated urgently, *"No."* He sounded as shaken as Megan felt. "That's not what I... I didn't want... I don't want your pity. God, that's the one thing I was trying to avoid, back then."

"Then what *do* you want?" Megan could have groaned; her voice sounded so tiny, so tremulous. She was conscious only of the fact that he was touching her, conscious only of the searing heat of his hands on her shoulders. She sucked in a quick breath, strangely afraid for a moment that there wasn't enough air in the room.

He was staring at her, and she couldn't seem to move no matter how loudly her mind was screaming at her to get away from that alluring, tempting touch. Neither could she look away; as it had been six years ago, his eyes held her in a way she'd never known before him, and never since.

She knew in the instant before he moved that he was going to kiss her. She also knew she was a fool not to stop him. Hadn't she proved that day at the site that she was as vulnerable to him as ever? Hadn't she shown him she still went up in flames at his touch? And then his mouth was on hers, his lips soft, warm and coaxing, and the surging response of her body drowned out the last, flimsy protests of her mind. This was the only man who had ever moved her, the only man, she thought despairingly, who ever would.

Then there was no room for thought, not when his tongue was stroking her lips, not when his hands slid up to cup her face, not when she could feel the strong, hot length of him so close to her. And when his tongue probed gently, she could do nothing but part her lips for him.

She heard the sound he made, low and rough, from deep in his throat. It sent little rockets of fire through her already heated blood. And when he drew back, when he took that sweet, honeyed heat away from her, she gave a little moan of protest. Then it was her tongue probing, testing. God, he tasted so good...so hot... He was drawing her in deeper and deeper, and she couldn't stop it. Didn't want to stop it. She was feeling, really feeling, for the first time in so very long, and her instinctive joyous response drowned all caution.

She was only vaguely aware of his hands moving, sliding down her arms, along her ribcage, only vaguely aware of her own movement, of the way she was pressing herself to him, needing his heat, his strength, only vaguely aware of anything other than the growing, spiraling stream of sensation. Then his hands found the outer curve of her breasts and his fingers curled to cup and hold her. She twisted her body, seeking, and as if he knew exactly what she needed, his fingers brushed over the already tightened peaks.

Megan gasped, the pleasure that swamped her stealing her breath away. And then, over the pulse pounding in her ears, over Dev's suddenly harsh breathing, she heard another sound. Kevin. Her son. His son.

With a sudden, almost violent movement, she twisted out of his grasp. Her body cried out in protest, wanting more of the sweetness it had been waiting six years to feel again. But Megan ignored the ache growing inside her and wrapped her arms around herself, even as she acknowledged the futility of the action; nothing would ever feel like Dev's arms around her.

"What—" She broke off, swallowing tightly, hating the way her voice sounded, breathless and husky. She tried again to repeat her earlier question, aware that this time it had taken on even more meaning. "What do you want from me?"

Dev stared at her, then at his hands, the hands that had caressed her so sweetly. Slowly he lifted them, turning them to look at his palms as if they belonged to someone else. Once again his fingers curled, and his fists were jammed back into his pockets. He backed a step away from her, then another, as if the first hadn't put a safe enough distance between them. Megan was grateful; it gave her a chance to pull herself together.

"I want..." Dev's voice trailed off, and she saw a shiver ripple through him. He drew in a deep breath, as if he needed to steady himself as much as she had after that searing kiss. That breath caught audibly in his throat as his gaze lowered; Megan crossed her arms defensively over her still tingling breasts, knowing her nipples, taut and aroused, were what had caught his eye. And knowing, from the new tightness of the front of his jeans, that he was just as aroused as she was did nothing to ease her confusion.

It was a long, strained moment before he at last spoke. "I just wanted you to maybe understand." He stopped, looking at her. He took one step forward, then halted, as if reminding himself of a danger zone. With a visible effort, he went on. "Can you understand? Can you believe that I never once thought that you might be pregnant?"

Megan gasped. "No, I told you..." she began desperately.

"I know. He's not mine. But he could have been. God, he could have been, and I never once even considered it."

Nearly reeling in her relief, Megan tried to concentrate on what he was saying, the effort putting an edge in her voice. "It's... a little late to be worrying about that, isn't it?"

He answered softly, as if he hadn't heard the sharpness of her tone. "Much too late. But I *couldn't* consider it, Meg. I couldn't. The thought of you pregnant, with my baby, would have been the last straw. If I'd thought about that, if I'd let myself think for even a second..." He looked away and shuddered, a small ripple that Megan almost felt herself. "I would have broken, Meg. I could never have carried that, too. Any more than I could have faced you and ended the only thing that was letting me hang on to the rest."

Megan stared at him, seeing the helplessness he'd felt then, the shame he was feeling now. "Dev..."

His head came up. "So I didn't," he said flatly, meeting her gaze. "I simply didn't consider it. My mind went on automatic and pushed the possibility back into some dark corner. Until today."

His gaze flicked back toward the family room once more, then back to Megan. She saw the long-ago shadows, haunting the hazel eyes once more. He took a shaky breath.

"If you *had* been pregnant, you could have come to me. I would have..." He ended on a helpless shrug, as if he really didn't know what he would have done.

"After I found out you were married?" Megan asked harshly. "Your silence and absence made it quite clear how welcome I would be," she added, unable to stop the bitterness from echoing in her voice.

"I had so many damned people depending on me," he said with a weary shake of his head. "My family. Hers. And I'd just started Cross Consulting, I couldn't desert the company, or the people who opened it with me, not when it was just getting started. And there were the bills..."

Megan smothered a start of realization. *Short money blues*, he'd said. And that it was personal, not business. Lord, could he still be digging out from under his wife's medical bills? It was possible, she thought. Probable. He'd never had much to spare in San Diego; he'd been on a budget nearly as tight as hers. It would explain why he was still driving the Jeep. And why, according to Frank Mason, he worked sixteen hours nearly every day.

"Sometimes," he said, his voice rough, "I felt if I broke, they'd all fall apart. It was like I was holding them all together. I couldn't let them all down, Meg. I just couldn't."

Megan clamped down on the wave of sympathy she felt welling up inside her. She wondered if she would have been able to do it, had it not been for the child in the other room. But nothing changed the fact that she had been so alone during that horrible time, and that her son had never known a father.

"You couldn't let them down," she repeated softly, hating the fact that she sounded so wounded. "So you let me down instead."

When she saw the look of anguish that flashed across his face, Megan almost regretted the words. Only the sound of

Kevin's voice from the other room steadied her. Then the look was gone, and his face was carefully impassive.

"I only came back," he said formally, "to apologize for not thinking about all the possibilities. I was irresponsible not to protect you in the first place, and more so not to make sure you weren't pregnant afterward. I don't expect you to understand why, I just wanted you to know that I'm sorry. Very sorry."

He moved jerkily, heading toward the door. Then he stopped, and half turned to look back at her.

"I regret that night, Meg, but only for what it did to you, and because I took what I had no right to." She saw him swallow, as if his throat was tight. "I used to remember that night, when it seemed like there was nothing left, when I wanted to go out and drive off the Coronado bridge. It hurt so much, knowing what I'd done to you, but as much as it hurt, it was . . . it was the most incredible night I've ever known. And it saved my life."

He turned away almost sharply, and was out of the room and gone before Megan could react. She heard the front door open and close, and was still standing motionless in the drawing room when she heard the Jeep's engine start and the sound of it leaving.

Megan sank down into one of the brocade-upholstered wing chairs, only then aware that her legs were trembling. And her hands, too, she noticed idly, as if from a distance. She studied them, the long, slender fingers, practical, rounded, polished nails, studied them as if she'd never seen them before.

She knew what her mind was doing, seizing on the mundane to avoid dealing with her rioting emotions, but it didn't help. She couldn't stop.

It was much later, as she sat alone in the darkened study after tucking Kevin into bed, that she at last was forced to confront her whirling thoughts. Adding to her pain was

Kevin's sleepy admission that he had liked the man who had helped him without making him feel dumb.

She was so tired of all the ugly memories. She didn't want to see them, but they were there, so close to the surface that she could no longer avoid them. Hurt, shock, betrayal, anger—they were all present, seemingly as strong in retrospect as they had been in reality.

Strong enough to make her cry when she had sworn she never would again, Megan thought in disgust, wiping at her damp eyes. She reached over and flicked on the small desk lamp, because the darkness only made the unwanted memories more vivid, more intense.

If he'd believed that Kevin was not his son, what did he want from her? Forgiveness? Absolution? She sighed. Maybe she was provincial, but she'd had her parents' example to show her the way. They'd been utterly, completely faithful, but then again, they'd never had to face what Dev had faced. When her mother had died, it had happened quickly, mercifully. But did his wife's traumatic death justify what Dev had done?

What *they* had done, she amended. She had long ago admitted that she shared the guilt for that night. Maybe she hadn't known the truth, but she'd had no business falling so hard and so fast for a man that, despite the months she'd known him, she really knew so little about. She'd been the foolish child her father had called her, too ignorant to even recognize the obvious signs. His reticence, his silences, his hesitancy at ever seeing her anywhere except at the coffee shop or at her apartment, never meeting his friends. Looking back she could only shake her head at her own naïveté.

Unbidden an image rose before her, of her father tied helplessly to a hospital bed, neither dead nor alive, of herself trying to keep his work going while she reassured and took care of Kevin, while she tried to prop up the rest of the family, Uncle James, her cousins, all of her father's many friends. She pictured trying to deal with the certain out-pouring of sympathy and pity, the incredible pressure, the helplessness . . .

If someone came along, someone away from it all, some-one who made her feel hope, or at least saved her for a time from all of the pain, could she honestly say she would walk away? Even if it was wrong?

She didn't know. When dawn broke hours later, filling the room with a dim, gray light that matched her confusion, she was still sitting there, wondering. And she still didn't know. But there was one thing she did know. No matter how many times she called herself a fool, she couldn't bring herself to wish he hadn't kissed her.

Six

Dev fiddled with the pencil he held, not really seeing it, or the papers spread out over his desk. He didn't need to look at them again; he knew perfectly well what they said. The new set of core samples he'd taken were as bad, at least from the Mason Development point of view, as the others had been. He didn't relish breaking the news to the touchy Frank Mason.

He got up, walking over to the window of the office. There wasn't much to see, except taller buildings, here in this commercial zone near the busy freeway. It wasn't like the pleasant expanse of trees and small buildings and houses that spread out to the ocean from the window of the office in San Diego.

It hadn't mattered when he'd first come here. He'd been glad to get away, to leave the city that held so many painful memories. Memories of a young woman dying before her time, of a shattered life... and of Meg, and what he'd done to her. And then, just when he'd thought he could be free of those memories for a while, he'd walked into a crowded room and collided with his painful past.

For the first time he began to wish that he'd let Jeff handle this. His partner had offered, but Dev had sensed his heart really wasn't in it. They both knew that this was going to be a one-man operation until they found out if this expansion was going to work, and that that one man was going to be putting in some long hours.

"We've got a good staff here in San Diego, plenty of help," Dev had told him. "You can go home at night and help Linda with the baby. You know she won't want you to go alone, and she doesn't want to move at this stage, either. There's no sense in disrupting your home life when we don't know whether this is going to fly or not."

Jeff Russell had looked at him knowingly. "So you'll disrupt yours instead."

Dev had shrugged, avoiding Jeff's perceptive gaze. They both knew that his work was his life, and that home was just someplace he went in between.

"When are you gonna slow down, Dev? You've got to get off this merry-go-round you've put yourself on sometime. It's been nearly five years now. You can't go on like this forever, you—"

"Knock it off, Russell," he said gruffly. "We've got one mother hen around here already. We don't need another one."

"Mrs. Harris is not a mother hen. It just seems that way sometimes because she's been around so long. And don't try to change the subject."

"I'm not changing it. I'm dropping it."

"Dev—"

"Make that, *we're* dropping it."

"Damn it, Dev—"

"I'll handle opening the Orange County office."

Jeff knew that tone in his old classmate's voice, and sighed in resignation. "All right, all right. But at least take Matt or Luis with you to help with the field work."

"I can handle it."

"I never said you couldn't. I know better. You built this place up from nothin', didn't you? When everyone said you should stick with Gordon and Sons? And you took me on when I couldn't hack the three-piece-suit bit. I owe you, my friend."

"No," Dev said tightly, thinking of all the times Jeff had been there for him when he needed it most. All the times his friend had forced him to come out of hiding and face the world, all the times he'd pulled him back from the very brink of despair. "No," he said again, "you don't owe me a thing. Stay home with your family. I'll handle it."

"Damn it, buddy, you can't keep this up forever. How long are you going to—" He broke off as Dev eyed him warningly. "Okay, okay. No more lectures. Just promise me you'll holler for help if you need it. I can be up there in a couple of hours."

"I will."

"I wish I believed that," Jeff had muttered, but he'd dropped the subject.

He was about ready to call in that offer, Dev thought as he stared out at the busy street below the two-story office building that was dwarfed by the towering glass high rises around it. Frank Mason was, in addition to being one of the biggest developers in Southern California, simply becoming a pain to work with.

Dev supposed being somewhat of a steamroller had gotten the man where he was, but it was a more than irritating trait to have to deal with. The man was constantly pushing to expedite every phase of the project, as if each inevitable delay was a personal affront, and the slightest hint of another sent him bouncing off the walls.

Jeff could handle that. Jeff was better at dealing with that kind of person than he was. His laid-back, casual manner seemed infectious when he turned on that Texas charm. A charm, Dev had learned early in their first year of college together, that hid a razor-sharp mind.

Yes, Jeff would be able to handle Frank Mason, Dev thought. He'd have him soothed and adopting a Texas drawl inside of an hour, and Mason would never know what hit him. And Jeff would definitely be a lot more at ease at this luncheon Mason was dragging him to Friday.

Friday. *Today.* It hit him with a thud, and he jerked his left arm up to look at his watch. *Damn.* He was going to have to make tracks if he was going to be there on time. He grabbed his lightweight jacket, the only concession necessary to the mild California winter, and quickly locked up the office.

He'd been wary of going to this event—so wary, he realized, that he had nearly forgotten it altogether—but Mason insisted that he fill the last seat of the table he was sponsoring. "Always buy a table for the Police Awards," he'd said. "It's good for the company image, keeps the Chamber of Commerce on my side."

"I'm sure it does," Dev had said, smiling ruefully at himself for thinking, just for a minute, that Mason might have wanted only to support his local police force.

Dev knew, of course, that with her father speaking, Megan would be there. It was both what had made him reluctant to come and what had finally decided him, although even now he was having second thoughts. After her reaction to his strained explanations and apologies, he felt a little like a mouse too stupid to stay away from the cheese-baited trap, but he didn't seem to have any choice.

He wondered, as he drove southbound toward the Pacific glistening in the distance under the winter sun, if he was making a mistake. A big one. Again. He would not be welcomed, he told himself, not by Megan Spencer. Any softening he'd sensed in her had been from the pity he'd tried so hard to avoid, not from any feeling for him.

Still, searching for some sign that he was wrong, he played every encounter with her over in his head, again and again. He studied every expression that had changed the careful mask that had taken the place of the lively, expressive face he'd once known.

That alone, that he had been able to shake that polished, practiced expression, gave him a forlorn hope. And no matter how he tried, he couldn't seem to quash it. She might be angry, she might even despise him, but she wasn't indifferent to him. A small, perhaps bitter crumb of comfort, but enough, he thought, for now. It was a place to start.

A place to start. He sat staring at a red traffic light without seeing it. Why had he thought that? He intended to leave her alone, as she'd made it clear she wanted him to, didn't he? Then why was he thinking of a place to start? Did he intend to start? To try, even though she hadn't forgiven him, might not ever forgive him? Even knowing the chances were excellent that she'd reject him in an instant?

The thought made him cringe inwardly, then he laughed at himself; he was thinking like he had something to lose. If she rejected him, where would he be? Right where he was. A little more tattered, maybe, but he was so ragged now it wouldn't matter. Still, the idea startled him, and he kept turning it over in his mind.

A honk from behind him startled him out of his unexpected contemplation, and he yanked the wheel of the Jeep as he turned the corner. And shoved the tempting idea of having Meg in his life again out of his mind. Which is what you are, he told himself sardonically. Out of your mind for even thinking like that. For even showing your face to her again. It was, he thought sourly, going to be a long afternoon.

* * *

"Megan, love, who *is* that man?"

Megan toyed with the elaborately folded napkin that sat on the plate before her. "What man?" she asked, although she knew perfectly well who Susan Harper was referring to. She'd known he was there from the moment he'd walked into the huge banquet room, and she had felt his eyes on her ever since.

"The one who's been staring at you, of course. You can't not have noticed."

Megan lifted her gaze to meet the warm, brown eyes of the woman who sat beside her. She liked Susan Harper, she thought, not for the first time. The woman had worked for her father for years, running his office in Sacramento. She was, in effect, Megan's counterpart in the capitol. She was a pleasantly rounded woman of fifty-five, charming and vivacious, her beautifully silver hair an asset rather than the impediment some might think it.

She was also much too smart to be fooled. Megan sighed inwardly. "He works for Frank Mason. We've met a couple of times recently." She hoped the older woman would accept the implication that it had been their first meeting.

"Well, he seems quite entranced, I must say."

Megan couldn't think of a thing to say, so she merely shrugged.

"Of course, you are looking particularly lovely today."

Megan smiled rather thinly, although she knew the compliment was genuine. She'd come to know that Susan was as honest and open as she looked, although she could summon up an icy sharpness when it was necessary, something which made the woman invaluable to her father.

She might even, if she hadn't been so uncertain about everything lately, have believed the compliment. She'd taken extra care, telling herself it was so she would look worthy of her father, and not because the thought that Dev might be at Frank Mason's table had occurred to her. Not, of course, that she cared one way or the other if he was.

She just wanted to look her best, she assured herself yet again. And she knew she looked more than presentable. The suit she wore was a pale blue rough-textured silk, with a short double-breasted jacket that nipped in at the waist over a slim, straight skirt that was short enough to bare shapely knees without being blatant. She'd worn matching high-heels, and the small but exquisite teardrop-shaped blue topaz necklace her father had given her for her twenty-first birthday sparkled at her throat.

She didn't think she'd consciously chosen that necklace for any other reason than that the stone went wonderfully with the suit. Only after she'd donned it had she remembered the day when, on one of the long walks she and Dev had taken, she'd spotted a display of some lovely topazes in a store window. She had always loved the clear, light blue stones, and had stopped to look.

"They're beautiful. The same color as your eyes," Dev had said.

It tightened her throat unbearably, as he so rarely said things like that. She couldn't speak, so desperately was she hugging his words to herself, as she did any slight sign that he might care beyond just a casual friendship. She couldn't look at him, sure he would see the love glowing in her face, but she kept her eyes fastened on the faint reflection of him in the store's window.

"You should have those," he said suddenly, almost angrily. "You should be with someone who can give them to you."

Aware of his sudden tension, she chose her words carefully. "I'd rather have someone I love."

In the glass she saw him close his eyes as if in pain, then heard him let out a long breath. "Be careful of who you love, Meggie. Make sure they deserve it first."

Now she touched the cool stone at her throat, fingering the curve of the golden setting as she wondered whether she'd subconsciously worn it because of that day.

She heard the bustle as her father, having run the gauntlet of the throng of people who wanted to greet him, made it to their table just as the ceremony began. She pulled herself back to the present, resolutely determined to ignore the feel of Dev's eyes on her. He'd made no effort to approach her, but then it would have been difficult in the crush around the senator's table.

It went, she thought, smoothly. Her father's speech—her words, but delivered with his own special flair—was well received. Megan watched the award presentations, trying to appreciate the hours of dedicated police work that had earned them, and applauding the heroics that had won a Medal of Valor. The only problem was, she kept finding herself thinking that none of these men, who dealt with the more rotten side of humanity day after day, looked as haunted as Dev had the first time she'd seen him.

When it was over, she knew better than to get up; her father would be holding court for at least another hour, if not more. Susan gave her a commiserating smile; she also knew how this worked all too well. But the smile changed when the woman looked at something over Megan's shoulder, and her quick brown eyes flicked to Megan's. Megan was thankful for the warning, it gave her time to compose her expression before the deep, husky voice came, greeting her father respectfully.

"Ah, Dev, I was hoping you'd stop by," Harlan said jovially. "Meet Susan Harper, my right hand in Sacramento. Susan, Dev Cross. He's working with Frank Mason on the Gold Coast project."

Susan smiled in acknowledgment, and Dev nodded gravely, his gaze flicking to Megan. She saw his eyes widen, then narrow as they took in the soft blue of the necklace. Then he looked back to her father.

"You have excellent taste in both cities, sir."

Megan couldn't stop her shocked look as her father chuckled and Susan, surprisingly, blushed. Where had this debonair charmer come from?

"Sit down for a minute with us. I've been trying to get ready for a State Coastal Commission meeting in the capitol next week. They have a similar project on the north coast before them, and Susan tells me they're going to be armed to the teeth with questions on the Gold Coast project."

Dev looked doubtful, and glanced over his shoulder to where Frank Mason was heartily clapping a local city councilman's shoulder. "I'm just the geologist. Mr. Mason would be the person to ask."

"Frank gives whatever version of the truth is going to get the results he wants," Harlan said dryly.

"Which is probably why he gets what he wants most of the time," Dev said, then looked as if he regretted the words.

But Harlan laughed, and Megan saw the sparkle in his eyes that told her he was enjoying this. "I knew I liked you. Sit down," he repeated, "and tell me how I can explain to the people in Sacramento that what works here won't necessarily work up there. They can't seem to realize that it's almost a different world here."

Dev glanced once more at Megan. She kept her expression carefully neutral, and after a moment he took the proffered chair.

"Not almost. Is. Geologically, Southern California literally *is* a different world."

Harlan raised an eyebrow. "Oh? How so?"

"The whole surface of the earth is divided into plates of land. Seven major ones. Southern California is on the Pacific tectonic plate. Northern California and the rest of the country is on the North American plate." Dev shrugged. "They're all in constant motion. The twain meet, and sometimes bounce, but don't mix."

The silver brows furrowed. "Bounce?"

"Yes. In places like that little crack called the San Andreas Fault."

Harlan sat back, an odd look on his face. Susan stared at Dev. "I've never heard it explained so clearly," she said. "Scientists always clutter it up with complicated language, so that all you're sure of is that we've had an earthquake. You should be a teacher."

Megan had to bite her lip to keep her expression from changing. Dev's gaze flicked to her, and she saw the same memories of other lessons reflected in the hazel eyes. He looked away before anyone noticed that split second of silent communication.

"I have to keep it simple," he told Susan with a smile, "so *I* can understand it. If it gets any trickier, I turn it over to my partner. He's the seismology expert."

"Is your partner as tactful in explaining to the ignorant public?" Susan asked with a smile that told Megan she, too, was enjoying this.

Dev's mouth twisted ruefully. "He's much better than I am. He's a downright charmin' Texan, ma'am."

Susan laughed, Harlan chuckled, and even Megan found herself smiling at the assumed drawl. He *had* changed, she thought. He wasn't exactly happy, his eyes were still too weary for that, but he seemed less driven; the old Dev had been too weighted down to tease like this. Without thinking, she looked at Dev and asked simply, "Jeff?"

His gaze darted to her father, then back to her. Although Jeff hadn't yet become his partner when he'd met Megan, Dev had told her about him one day when they'd tired of going over the Wentworth scale of rocks for the umpteenth time.

Megan's cheeks flamed suddenly as she realized what she had done. But Dev spoke quickly, saving her from any further embarrassment.

"Yes," he said smoothly, "I'm sure Frank mentioned him to you the other day." He shifted his gaze to her father. "And I'm sure you don't need any help in persuading anyone, sir."

He had successfully diverted any speculation her inadvertent slip might have caused. Silently, fervently, Megan thanked him. And felt a spark of the old anger—she didn't want to soften towards him, it was too dangerous. But she couldn't seem to fan the spark into a flame, and she wondered if it was dying out altogether. A frightening idea, when she thought about the other kind of sparks that all too easily leapt into flame when she was around Devlin Cross.

"I wish it were true," Harlan was saying.

"You know you're a born speaker, Harlan," Susan said. "Why, look at how they responded here today."

"That was thanks to my speech writer," the senator said with a smile for his daughter. "She—"

"—is looking enchanting, as usual." With the inevitable cigar—thankfully unlit in this no-smoking room—clenched between his teeth, Frank Mason pulled out the one remaining empty chair and sat down. He grinned at Dev, then leaned back expansively. "Thanks for keeping my boy here entertained. I must say, you have better luck than I do. He's always so damned serious when I'm around. Can't hardly get a word out of him, except to give me bad news."

"Bad news?" Susan asked, eyeing the cigar balefully, as if she feared he was going to light it at any moment.

Mason snorted. "Gonna make me compact every foot of that project. Costing me an arm and a leg, in time and money."

"Compact?" Harlan shifted his gaze to Dev. "Can I have another simple explanation?"

"The soil in that area isn't solid enough to bear the weight of the kind of load we're talking about. So you have to compact it." At Harlan's look, he went on. "You dig it out, mix it with water and whatever else it takes, put it back and compress it until it's as close to solid as you can get."

"Ninety-eight-percent solid," Mason said sourly. "Damned nuisance. Thing would have held."

"Maybe."

"It would," Mason said positively. "Bureaucrats. Never built a doghouse, but they think they know it all. Yourself excluded, of course, Harlan," he amended quickly.

"I never have built a doghouse," Harlan said mildly. Dev smothered a smile. "But then, that's why I hire experts like Dev to tell me what I don't know. And I listen to their advice."

The reproof in his words was subtle, but Mason got it. He looked aggrieved. His point tactfully made, Harlan didn't dwell on it.

"I just wish they all made as much sense as he does," he said, smiling at Dev.

Mason muttered something, then walked off as he spotted one of his investors across the room. The man, a local banker Megan vaguely recognized, didn't look at all happy. Maybe he was afraid the noxious cigar was lit, she thought. The man listened to Mason for a moment, his expression darkening, and Mason hastily ushered him away toward a more private corner of the room.

"So, *would* it hold?" her father asked Dev.

"Maybe." He met the senator's steady gaze as he repeated his answer. "But I wouldn't want to bet the lives of the guests of that hotel on a maybe."

Something akin to a salute flashed in the blue eyes that were so like Megan's, and Harlan Spencer nodded like a man who has just had his judgment confirmed.

"You're going to be in town for a while, aren't you?" he asked Dev.

Dev's brow creased slightly, but he nodded.

"Good. I'm leaving in a few days for a couple of weeks in Sacramento, but I promised I'd be back in time for the birthday party my daughter insists on throwing for me. It will be at the Aliso Beach Country Club, on the twentieth. Formal, I'm afraid, but if you're free, I'd like you to come."

Taken aback, Dev gaped at him. The senator merely smiled. "I don't meet many people who talk as straight as you do. When I do, I like having them around."

"I..."

Dev trailed off, turning to look at Megan. She had recovered from her shock at her father's words and realized ruefully that she should have expected this. She knew Dev was waiting for her to do or say something to stop it. She read in his eyes the uncompromising admission that she, of all people, knew how wrong her father was about him. And in that moment she knew, starkly and unarguably, that he had suffered just as much as she had in the last six years.

"Fine," she said suddenly, almost involuntarily. "I have plenty of time to add one to the guest list."

She was aware that Dev was staring at her, sensed that he was trying not to read anything into her unexpected acquiescence. She could almost see the moment when he decided that she'd only agreed because she had no choice. And he was right, she told herself. To argue would be to raise questions she didn't want to answer. And she managed to keep herself convinced of that until the moment when she was at last alone, curled up in the big brass bed in her room.

She'd often thought of moving out of this house, and others had often asked her why she still lived at home at age twenty-five. But it seemed much easier, and more practical, when her father was gone so often and so much of the work was done out of his office here. And this was where she'd run to when her world had crumbled, this had been the lair she'd bolted to to lick her wounds. When she'd been trying to convince herself she hated Devlin Cross with all her battered heart.

Was she starting to forgive him? At last, there in the darkness, she faced the question that had been hovering since she'd first learned the truth about what had happened six years ago. Was she? Or was it just that enough time had passed, that it truly didn't matter anymore?

No, she thought ruefully, if it didn't matter he wouldn't be able to throw her into this state of constant confusion, she who had spent those six years building her control and her composure into an unshakable facade. He wouldn't be able to tug at emotions long buried. And most of all, he wouldn't be able to fire her blood with a look, a touch. No, it mattered. It mattered too much.

He loved her. The words he'd said in the trailer that day echoed in her ears, sending her heart racing. He'd said it at last, even if it was years too late. And he'd loved her six years ago. He hadn't said it then, because he wasn't free to. But did that make it right?

Her father had tried to tell her so many times in those days that not everything was black or white, but with the headstrong arrogance of youth she'd only half listened, and hadn't really believed at all. It had seemed so clear to her then. Right was right, wrong was wrong.

She'd learned since that her father had once again been right, and that in relationships in particular, there were two sides to every story. She'd never known Dev's side, had known nothing except that something was tearing him apart. But now that she did know, she wasn't sure it was any easier to deal with.

And what if she could forgive him? What if she could honestly say that she understood, that she could forgive him for what he'd done, considering the pressure he'd been under in that horrible time? What then?

She rolled over to her other side, kicking at the covers that were becoming tangled by her restless tossing. She tried to shut off the flow of tangled thoughts, to think of something else, anything else. She sat up suddenly, reached over and snapped on the bedside lamp. She walked to her bathroom, rinsed her face and burning, gritty eyes with cool water and walked back to the bedroom. Methodically she straightened the covers, tucking in the sheets where she'd kicked them free. She plumped the pillows, sat down and turned out the light once more.

With the grim determination that had gotten her through the cold, painful nights five years ago, she lay down once more and concentrated on going to sleep. She'd been a fool once, she told herself, but that didn't mean she had to be one again.

Seven

———

"—needed to talk to your father, damn it!"

Dev stopped in the doorway of the construction trailer, the latest core sample reports in his hand. He knew, even before he heard the answer to Mason's angry exclamation, who it was directed at. He glanced back over his shoulder at the gleaming yellow sports car parked next to Mason's Mercedes. He remembered now vaguely hearing the throaty purr of its motor the day she'd left him in a daze here at the trailer.

"I told you he sends his apologies. He sent me to see if I could help."

"Not unless you can pound some patience into those damned investors of mine!"

Dev tensed. Mason's tone made it clear he was close to another tirade. It had been worse, it seemed, since the hot Santa Ana winds had kicked up this week. Dev stepped inside just as Megan spoke again, a little stiffly.

"That's what you expected my father to do?"

"I expect him to care about this project, since it's going to make his district look so good," Mason said, his inflection a shade sarcastic. He saw Dev then, but gave him only a short nod. Meg saw the man's glance and turned. When she saw Dev, she seemed to draw back a little, although she recovered quickly and smoothly.

"My father cares a great deal about anything in his district," Megan said coolly to Mason. "That's why he's tied up in meetings with city mayors all day."

"Meetings," Mason snorted. "Bureaucratic bull—"

"Frank!" Megan cut him off sharply. "I would appreciate it if you would quit swearing in front of my son!"

Dev jerked in surprise, then looked around the interior of the trailer. Only then did he spot the small boy quietly sitting on the tall stool Dev frequently used himself, taking it all in with wide eyes.

Mason had the grace to look embarrassed. "Sorry. Look, I need to give you a message for Harlan." He glanced at Dev. "Dev, take the kid outside, will you? Show him a bulldozer or something."

"No," Megan said, so quickly Dev couldn't help wincing. She couldn't make it much clearer that she didn't want him anywhere near her son. Fine, he told himself. He wasn't sure he wanted to be anywhere around this reminder of how badly he'd messed up his life—and Meg's—anyway. And he certainly didn't want to stay here, not when she was standing there wearing that silky, clinging jumpsuit that made his blood heat from just looking at it, and at the way its deep blue color lit up her eyes.

"Why not?" Mason looked at Kevin with a smile that even the boy seemed to doubt. "You'd like to see all the big trucks, wouldn't you, son?"

When Kevin slowly nodded, Dev had an instinctive feeling it was more out of eagerness to get away from this tense scene than to look at heavy equipment. In either case, the boy looked at Megan hopefully.

"Can I, Mom?"

Megan hesitated.

"Let him go, Megan," Mason warned. "What I have to relay to your father won't be fit for his ears."

Then it's not fit for Meg's, either, Dev thought, but didn't voice it. She'd made it clear she didn't welcome his presence in her life; he knew she wouldn't appreciate his interference. He waited silently, seeing the quandary in her eyes even though her poised expression never changed. A gust of the hot Santa Ana wind rattled a window, but no one looked at it.

"Please, Mom?" Kevin seemed to be working up some enthusiasm for the idea now, but he hesitated, sliding Dev a shy, questioning glance. Dev couldn't help smiling back at the boy, who then went on eagerly, "I'd like to see that big digger thing."

Megan wavered. She looked from Kevin to Mason, then, at last, to Dev. Baby-sitting could hardly be listed as one of his responsibilities on this job, but he didn't protest. He wanted to know what Meg's decision would be. As if you don't know, he told himself harshly. She hardly has reason to trust you with anything, let alone her child.

"All right." Megan looked as surprised that she'd said it as Dev felt at hearing it. "Just be careful."

The short time they'd spent together working on the toy plane seemed to have alleviated any qualms Kevin had about him, and the moment his mother said yes he scrambled off the tall stool and ran across the room. Instinctively Dev held his hand out, and the boy took it without hesitation.

"I'll take care of him," Dev promised. It came out a little shakily. He wondered if it was because of his surprise that she'd agreed, or at the prospect of being alone with the child who could easily have been his own.

Megan didn't say anything more, but clear in her eyes was the memory that he had failed miserably to take care of *her* when he should have. Dev held her gaze, acknowledging the silent accusation, and her right to it. After a moment she looked away.

At the door, Dev paused for one more look at Meg. She was watching them, and he was startled by the sudden paleness of her face. Was she having second thoughts? Did she truly think he'd let anything happen to her son?

"I'll take care of him," he repeated. He turned back as Kevin scampered down the steps, overjoyed to be outside.

Dev heard Mason, not even waiting until they were out of earshot, snap out at Megan, "You tell Harlan that he'd damn well better help me get these guys off my back if he wants this—" the man spat out an obscene adjective "—project finished so he can show it off to his constituency."

Dev stopped, about to turn back and tell Mason to shut his filthy mouth. Then Megan, her poise obviously still shaken, did it for him.

"I will tell my father," she added angrily, "*exactly* what you said. I think that will be quite sufficient for him to judge for himself."

Mason took an audible breath, and when he went on, the practiced, cajoling tone was back.

"Now, Megan, honey, you know I was just blowing off steam. I'm under a lot of pressure here."

Dev had seen it before, Mason's realization that he'd gone too far. He would back off now, and be as soft as river silt until he smoothed things over. Knowing Meg was safe from any more of the man's invective, he continued down the steps to where Kevin was waiting patiently, blinking a little at the blowing dust.

"He sure gets mad, doesn't he?" the boy said.

Dev's mouth quirked. "Yeah, he sure does." Not sure why, he reached out and put a hand on the boy's thin shoulder. "What do you want to see first?"

"That digger thing," Kevin repeated enthusiastically. "The one that digs backwards, and goes real deep. You know, the one with the big claw on it!"

Dev grinned at the avid curiosity about rather violent-looking machinery. He gave the boy's shoulder a friendly pat.

"It's called a backhoe," he said. "Let's go see if I remember how to run one."

"Wow! Do you think I could ride it, Mr. Cross?"

Dev lifted a brow. "I thought we airplane builders were using first names."

The child made a face. "Mom said I have to call you Mr. Cross."

Dev smothered a wince. He fought down the twinge he felt at Meg's obvious effort to keep the distance between them. "Well, she's the boss. But I'm going to feel pretty silly calling you Mr. Spencer."

Kevin giggled, and Dev found himself grinning again at the sound of it.

"Come on," he said, tousling the boy's hair. "First thing you need is a hard hat."

"I do? Why? Is it really hard?"

Dev had always heard that kids were full of questions, but he'd never really experienced it firsthand. His nephew lived near Phoenix, and as close as that was, he rarely saw him. It hadn't been a conscious decision, just an awareness that being near his sister's happy family was acutely painful. He would, he thought as he tried to keep up with Kevin's bright, quick chatter, have to do something about that.

He felt like he'd given a crash course in trenching, grading and heavy equipment operation by the time the boy finally slowed down. He also felt an unexpected affinity. The boy who had at first seemed to him a symbol of all he'd done wrong in his life had become a person in his own right, a bright, intelligent child who soaked up information like loamy soil absorbed water.

Quitting time for the crews had long passed, and the wind had thankfully abated a little, when Dev glanced over and saw Meg coming out of the trailer at last. He began to lead the boy that way.

"Could I come back sometime?" Kevin asked wistfully.

"It's okay with me," Dev said, meaning it. "But it's really up to Mr. Mason . . . and your mother."

He nearly stumbled over the last part, but Kevin didn't seem to notice. "I'd like to come back," he said, looking over his shoulder to where the large earth mover sat parked. Then he looked back at Dev. "How'd you learn all this stuff?"

"College," Dev said.

"Oh." The boy's face fell. "I don't want to go to college." He looked at Dev hopefully. "Did you have to go for a long time to learn about— What are they?"

"Backhoes," Dev supplied, smiling. "I sort of picked that up after I graduated." He studied the boy walking beside him for a moment. "You don't want to go to college?"

"I don't think it's a very fun place," Kevin said. "It makes you sad."

"College makes you sad?"

"It made my mom sad," the child said with certainty.

Dev stopped dead. Kevin did, too, looking up at him curiously.

"College made your mom sad?" Dev asked carefully. Kevin nodded. "How do you know that?"

"Because," Kevin explained solemnly, "she's been lookin' at the pictures she drew there, and it makes her cry."

Dev sucked in a short, deep breath at the pain that swept through him. The searing emotion was followed by a flare of that old, seemingly unquenchable hope. Did she still have some feeling for him, something besides the hatred he knew she must feel?

He heard Meg call to Kevin across the few feet that separated them, and barely managed to shake off his tangled emotions long enough to nod at the boy's hasty goodbye.

"Thanks, Mr. Cross!" Kevin called out as he got into the car.

"My pleasure," he managed before Megan turned to look at him over the roof of the low sports car.

"Thank you for…looking out for him," she said at last, her voice oddly husky.

"I enjoyed it. He's a good kid."

"Yes. He is."

"Smart, too."

"Yes."

For a long moment they just stared at each other. When he sensed she was about to move, to get in the car to leave, he spoke quickly, not sure if he really wanted an answer or just wanted to stop her from going.

"Is he still in a frenzy?" he asked, gesturing toward the trailer.

"No." She glanced over her shoulder, as if to be sure the man they were discussing wasn't within hearing. "He always seems to know when he's gone too far." She glanced at the passenger seat, where her son was dutifully fastening his seat belt. "Thank you for taking Kevin out of there."

Dev shrugged. "You were right. He doesn't need to hear that kind of language." He smiled tentatively. "You shut him up, though."

Her cheeks pinkened. "I just get fed up with him sometimes. He's not so bad, usually. But he's pushing awfully hard for Dad to run interference for him."

"He's pushing hard, period," Dev said. "I think he's—"

He broke off as Mason came to the door of the trailer and bellowed, "Cross! I want to talk to you about these damn samples!"

With her back to Mason, Megan rolled her eyes. And melted Dev's heart with an unexpected smile of commiseration. Then, as if she'd caught herself and regretted the tiny overture, she said an abrupt goodbye and slid into the driver's seat. When the bright yellow car pulled away, Dev felt bereft, as if all the color in his own world had gone with it. Wondering how many more of these emotional ups and downs he could take, Dev trudged toward the trailer steps.

If Megan had had any thought of putting Dev out of her mind after leaving the site, Kevin buried it as surely as the heavy machinery buried the water pipe being laid in the trench running parallel to the construction road. He was chattering away, in the childishly random fashion that she usually enjoyed. Except that this time, one person kept popping up endlessly, it seemed.

"He took me for a ride on the digger, except it's really a backhoe—" he flashed a look at her, full of pride that he had remembered the word "—and he dug a hole with the claw end and then spun it around to scoop up the dirt with the other end and everything!"

"He...did?"

"Yeah!" He misinterpreted her hesitation, and hastened to assure her. "It was okay, Mom, he ran it, and made me just sit on his lap, with a seat belt, and I had to wear a hard hat, so my head couldn't get hurt. I thought it was sissy, but Dev—Mr. Cross wears one, too, so it's okay. And he showed me the tractors and graders and there was a bulldozer and the blade part was as tall as me, and—"

It went on and on, and Megan felt a tightness in her throat and a burning behind her eyelids at her son's enthusiasm. She had to blink rapidly to see the road as she drove. Had he missed a man's influence that badly? He had his grand-father, but Harlan was gone so much...

Or was it just Dev? God, was there some intangible link between father and son, some instinctive bonding that su-perseded ignorance of their relationship? Did they subcon-sciously sense that there was some connection between them? Why else would Dev take the time and make the ef-fort to be so good with a child he thought was hers by some man she'd run to the moment he turned his back on her? A shiver went through her as she pulled into the driveway of the house.

"—and he said I didn't have to call him Mr. Cross, but I told him you said I did, and he said you're the boss, so I did, but can I call him Dev now that we're friends?"

Megan gaped at her son, barely remembering to set the parking brake. "He said what?"

"He said I could call him Dev—"

"No, I mean about... the boss?"

"He said you were the boss, so we had to do what you said." Kevin giggled. "Then he called me 'Mr. Spencer.' Isn't that silly?"

"Yes," she whispered, trying hard to imagine the Dev she had known being silly. She couldn't. The Dev she'd known had been too haunted. But this Dev, being silly with his son... the thought took her breath away.

Kevin was still wound up when she tucked the boy into bed that evening.

"He said I could come back if I wanted," he enthused. "Can I, Mom?"

"I don't—"

"Please? He said it was really up to you and Mr. Mason, but it was okay with him."

"I won't say no, Kevin. But no promises. We'll see."

The boy made a face, even at age five acquainted with the vagaries of that parental "we'll see."

Pained confusion tightened Megan's throat as she kissed him goodnight and left the room. How was she supposed to deal with this? Once the Gold Coast job was finished, that would be the end of it, there would be no reason for Dev to tolerate a child with whom, to his knowledge, he had no connection. If she let Kevin spend more time with Dev, how would the boy feel when the inevitable happened, and Dev walked out of his life, just as he had walked out of hers?

You could tell Dev the truth.

The words floated up out of the depths of her consciousness, making her nearly stumble on the stairs. Tell Dev the truth? That Kevin was his son? That he had indeed left her pregnant when he had abandoned her after their one night together?

She shivered at the thought. And then smothered a tiny moan when she realized she wasn't sure if her fear of telling him was for her sake, or his. Once she might have relished the thought of hurting him as he had hurt her. But now, knowing the reasons behind what he'd done, she was no longer sure. Besides, she could never use Kevin as a weapon like that.

Needing the distraction of company, Megan found Mrs. Moreland in the family room, working on one of her inevitable pieces of needlework as she watched television.

"All tucked in?" the kindly woman asked as Megan sat down and picked up the newspaper.

"Yes, although I don't know how soon he'll sleep, what with the wind blowing. Plus he got awfully wound up today."

The woman smiled. "So I gathered. He seemed quite impressed with that nice Mr. Cross."

Megan kept her face carefully even. "Yes. He did."

"Young man like that's just the kind of example Kevin needs," Mrs. Moreland hinted broadly.

Megan's lips tightened, but she only shrugged. Mrs. Moreland had been with them for years, nearly twice Kevin's lifetime. The woman had practically raised Megan after her mother's death, and had been unwaveringly supportive when faced with the unexpected addition of a child to the household. Never once had she judged Megan, nor had she ever treated Kevin with anything less than unstinting kindness. Her own grandchildren were far away, and Megan knew that Kevin filled a need for Mrs. Moreland as much as she filled a need for the child, and Megan loved her dearly for her devotion.

"Young man like that wouldn't do you any harm, either," the housekeeper intoned solemnly.

Wouldn't do you any harm. Megan nearly groaned aloud at the irony of the well-intentioned words. For an instant, the truth, the whole painful story, hovered on her lips. She needed to talk, to share with someone, to try and find a way through the confusion.

"Everyone makes mistakes, honey," Mrs. Moreland said gently. "Don't let one ruin your whole life."

The woman so rarely brought up the subject that Megan knew it must be a sign of her own distracted state lately that she had now.

"I'm fine."

The response came automatically, and never had Megan been so aware that it was a lie. She was grateful when Mrs. Moreland put away her stitching and became engrossed in a movie. She was far from fine, and she knew it. She didn't think she'd ever felt so utterly confused, not even in the days after Dev had left her, not even when she'd discovered she was pregnant. Seeing Dev and Kevin together had been the final blow to her staggered mind, and no matter how hard she tried, she couldn't put the picture of Kevin running to Dev's outstretched hand out of her mind.

At last it became too much, and she retreated to the library. Seated at the desk, she pretended to look at the papers she'd taken from the tray on her father's desk. The faint plop as the first drop fell on the letter in front of her roused her to push the papers away, out of the way of the tears she could no longer stop.

When the doorbell rang, Megan blinked away the wetness and glanced at her watch. It was late, but couriers with messages for her father had come at odder hours than this, and no matter how little she wanted to face anyone, she knew she had no choice. She got up and headed for the door.

"I'll get it," she called to Mrs. Moreland as she passed the family-room door.

She really hadn't expected him this time, but as she stared at him standing there in the golden halo of her porch light, she realized she wasn't surprised. He seemed destined to haunt her in reality now as much as he'd haunted her memories for the last six years.

"Meg, I..."

He trailed off, one corner of his mouth twisting wryly as he failed to come up with any words to explain why he was here. Meg tilted her head, looking at him, waiting, wondering what on earth he expected of her.

The movement of her head sent the light from the porch fixture skittering over her wet cheeks. Dev went very still, staring at her. Slowly, he reached up to touch her, the backs of his fingers slipping over her tearstained skin with exquisite gentleness.

Suddenly, without quite knowing how, Megan was in his arms. He held her close, lifting one hand to press her head to his shoulder.

"God, Meg, I'm sorry. I just keep hurting you, don't I? I've hurt you so much already, and I'm still doing it. I never meant to, ever...."

She could feel him trembling, could hear the stark pain in his voice as it rumbled up from deep in his chest.

"It's okay," he murmured, tightening his hold on her; only then did she realize she, too, was trembling. "You don't have to cry anymore. I'll leave, and I swear I'll stay away. I'll get out of your life forever, Meggie, if that's what you want. Don't cry, please. You won't ever have to see me again."

"No!"

It broke from her on a choked little breath, and she felt Dev go rigid with surprise.

"Meg?" he whispered, sounding stunned.

No more stunned than she was, she thought, her mind still dazed by her instinctive response. Slowly Dev's hands went to her shoulders. He gripped them tightly, holding her even as he pushed her back so he could see her face.

"I thought that's what you wanted," he said, every word ringing with his effort to speak evenly, to rein in the violent hope she saw flaring in his eyes.

"I don't know what I want," she said miserably. "Except that I can't go on like this. I'm so confused all the time. It's like a roller-coaster ride—I'm in control one minute and a basket case the next...."

"Believe me," Dev said ruefully, "I understand."

"I can't live like this," she whispered. "I can't keep it all bottled up inside. I feel like I'm going to explode."

"Then don't," he said, suddenly urgent. "Let it out. Talk to me."

"To you?" She stared up at him incredulously. "You're the reason I feel this way!"

"I know that. That's why you need to talk to *me*. Get it all out, Meg." His mouth twisted ruefully. "Even if it's only to tell me what a jerk I am, it'll make you feel better."

"I'm not even sure of that anymore."

He closed his eyes for a moment, and she wondered if he hadn't if she would have seen that flare of hope again. When he opened them, his gaze was fastened on her. *"Talk to me, Meg,"* he urged. "Let's get it all out. Then, if you want me to, I'll walk away. And stay away."

"I don't know...."

"We've got to talk it through, Meg. Neither one of us can heal until we do. Besides," Dev added grimly, "who better to talk to than the fool who caused it all?"

She wavered, the urge she'd smothered earlier to share the load with someone, to try and work through the confusion, coming back full force. He seemed to sense her indecision, and spoke quickly.

"We'll go someplace neutral, Meg. Someplace where we won't be interrupted. And anytime you want to stop, I'll bring you home. No questions asked." He glanced through the open door of the house. "Is somebody here for Kevin?"

She nodded slowly, his concern touching her in a way that frightened her. "Mrs. Moreland's here."

Dev took a deep breath, then slowly let it out. "What do you say, Meg? Do we stop this roller coaster long enough to talk?"

When it came right down to it, Megan knew she had no choice. She'd meant it when she said she couldn't go on like this. And Dev was right, there were things that needed to be resolved before either of them could get on with their lives. Things that had been on hold far too long. She gave him a tremulous little nod, and after a quick word to Mrs. Moreland, she followed him outside.

Dev set the parking brake on the Jeep, then reached to turn off the ignition. The sound of the surf rolled up from the beach just below them, and the hulking shadowy shapes of several pieces of heavy equipment sat scattered behind them on the now silent construction site.

"I know you like the ocean," he said after a silent moment. "I thought we could take a walk. This part of the beach is blocked off because of the construction. Nobody will bother us.''

She nodded wordlessly and slid out of the Jeep. For a moment she looked back at the open vehicle, then tried to smooth back the strands that the wind had pulled from the neat twist of her hair.

''I'd forgotten how windy riding in this is.''

''Sorry. I guess I should have put the soft top on.''

He didn't mention that she'd never wanted him to before, that she had loved the open-air feel of the Jeep. He didn't have to; she knew he could see that she was remembering those rides as clearly as he was.

''No. It's all right.''

The silence was tense as they made their way down the bluff to the sand, not the tension of anger but of anticipation, as if neither of them knew what was going to come of this but felt it had to be done.

They walked to the waterline, the white foam swirling near their feet as the moonlit surf rolled in and then retreated. It was a long time before Dev came to a halt and turned to face her.

''Will you listen, Meg?'' he asked quietly. ''I know it's much too late, but will you?''

Slowly Megan nodded. They retreated from the wet sand and sat down in the shelter of a jagged rock. Dev seemed to brace himself, as if facing a dive from a towering cliff into unknown waters. It took him a long, silent moment to take the plunge.

''I... Maybe I should have told you from the start.'' He grimaced. ''At least I should have told you the minute I realized—'' He stopped, shook his head and dug his heels into the soft sand. ''Damn,'' he muttered, ''I had this all worked out, how to say it. God knows I had six years to practice it.'' He sucked in a long breath, then let it out in a sigh of disgust. "I want to tell you about everything, about that time…my marriage, everything. But I can't seem to start."

Something about long journeys starting with small steps flitted through Megan's mind, and she said neutrally, "What was her name?"

She saw him tense, then saw the taut muscles relax. "Elizabeth." It came softly, but fairly steadily. He turned to look at Megan. Then, as if the simple question had breached the dam built so long ago, he began to talk.

"She lived around the corner when we were kids. My sister used to baby-sit her—"

He broke off, and Megan knew her shock was evident. He has a sister, she thought numbly. My God, I didn't even know. A flash of that old, painful feeling of having been a complete fool went through her.

"I know," Dev whispered, reading her expression. "I'm sorry, Meggie."

"Go on," she said tightly.

His heels dug deeper into the sand. "Darlene—my sister—was five years older than me, and seven older than Elizabeth. Darlene used to bring her home sometimes when she was taking care of her. It seemed like Elizabeth was always around."

He stared out at the silvered sea as if it made it easier to talk if he didn't look at her. "Anyway, we spent a lot of time together. She was…like a little sister. She was an only child, so she kind of adopted us as family, because we were so close by." He gave a shrug of one shoulder. "I guess it made me feel good when she'd run to me if someone teased her or bothered her. Like a real big brother."

Megan felt an emotion she couldn't describe tugging at her as she pictured a young Dev fighting the neighborhood bully who'd dared pick on his "little sister."

"In high school she used to ride to school with me. She'd talk about the boys she liked, ask me about how guys think about things, and helped me try to figure out whatever crazy thing my girl of the moment had done. We just . . . talked."

He reached down to grab a handful of sand. "I didn't see her for a while after I graduated and went to UCSD. But when she started college, we started to run into each other again. Only it was different. She wasn't that little girl anymore. We . . . Well, we started to see each other again. And after she finished college, it seemed natural. To get married, I mean."

He let the sand slide through his fingers. The warm breeze caught it, sending it flying sideways. "Our parents tried to talk us out of it. I'd just broken away from Gordon and Sons to start my own company, and they thought it would be too much. But we did all right."

Megan didn't think she made a sound, but he turned his head as if she had.

"I won't lie to you and say I didn't love her. I did."

"I wouldn't want you to lie," she said quietly. "In fact, I think I'd be more upset if you did. It would mean you didn't consider me important enough to know the truth, or that you married someone you didn't love."

He stared at her, his eyes searching her face in the moonlight. His hands came up as if to reach for her, then he curled his fingers back against his palms and dropped his arms to his sides.

"You haven't lost it," he whispered. "That way of making sense out of—"

He stopped, pulling away, and leaned back against the rock behind them. His shoulders stiffened, as if he were again picking up a heavy burden that had been set down for a moment.

"I loved her," he repeated. "I'm just not sure it was the kind of love you should get married for. But I wasn't sure there *was* another kind. Then." His eyes were fastened on her unwaveringly this time, and she understood that he knew it now. "I think we both knew something was...missing, I guess, but we put off doing anything about it. We were comfortable."

For a moment that old, weary, haunted look glimmered in the hazel eyes. When he went on, his voice was thick, as if forced past a very tight throat. "I think I knew we should have stayed just friends when I realized that it was the friendship I missed the most, afterward...."

"Ever since you told me," Megan said softly, "I've tried to imagine what it must have been like for you."

"You couldn't. I don't think anyone could. It was hell. I was at the hospital every day, for hours. And trying to keep the company on its feet, without taking the jobs I needed to."

"Needed to?"

Dev ran a hand through his wind-tousled hair. "The ones that pay the best are the ones that are the farthest out. I turned down chances to make some big bucks going to Arabia, Alaska, South America. But I couldn't leave, not with Elizabeth like that. So all the time the bills were mounting, I was getting deeper in the hole." He sighed. "Jeff kept trying to get me to ease up. He said I couldn't hold everybody together. But I had to try."

For Megan, it all came rushing back as if it had been only yesterday. Dev's haunted eyes, the lines of exhaustion grooved into a too-young face, and the sensation she'd so often had that he was fighting himself.

He shifted, his eyes fastening on her steadily. "Then I found a life preserver. Something that gave me the strength to keep going, to hang on, even though all I wanted to do was collapse. You, Meg. You're the only thing that kept me going."

"God, I wish you'd told me!" It burst from her raggedly.

"I told you, I couldn't. I needed you so much. I know it sounds like some big macho thing, but you made me feel like I wasn't totally helpless, like I was still some kind of a man at least."

"Oh, Dev, how could you ever think—"

"Because everybody I knew looked at me as if I were some wounded animal, as if I were something they had to help out of pity, but didn't like being around because it made them uncomfortable. It was Elizabeth who was suffering, but it was *me* they felt sorry for."

His thick lashes lowered as he looked down at the sand. "So I was selfish. Purely selfish. I wanted one place, one part of my life, untouched by all the rest. And I ended up hurting the one person who gave me the strength to keep going. I never would have made it.... And even then, all I could do was nothing. Just sit and wait. And that's exactly what I did."

"Dev, stop." She couldn't bear it anymore, and in a strange way the pain she felt for him and what he'd been through expanded to include the woman she'd never known. "Don't disparage what you went through. It was hell. For you, as well as Elizabeth. Belittling it diminishes the both of you."

He stared at her. Then he shook his head slowly. "Meggie... God, how do you do it? How can you... After what I did to you..." He smothered a groan. It was a moment before he went on. "I just felt so damned guilty. I wasn't there when she got hit, I was off on some job in Mexico."

"Dev, it was a drunk driver. You couldn't have done anything if you had been there."

"I know that. It took me two years to finally figure it out. And by then, by the time I shook that guilt, I met you." His jaw tightened. "And then I found out what it really meant to feel guilty."

"Oh, Dev." He was right, she thought. She couldn't begin to understand what he'd been through.

"You know what's really crazy?" he said, an odd look coming over his face. "I kept feeling that I needed to talk to somebody about it, about you, about how screwed up I was getting. But the only person I could think of that would understand was my best friend. The one I used to complain to about this girl or that one. The one who used to cry on my shoulder about boys being such idiots."

"Elizabeth," Megan said softly.

"Yeah." He shook his head. "Crazy," he repeated.

"No. You said that you'd found you missed the friendship the most."

"Yes." He reached up to run a hand through his tousled hair again. "Elizabeth said once that she wondered if we'd ruined a perfectly good friendship. Maybe we did. We never really had the chance to find out."

His voice dropped to a husky whisper. "All I really know is, I never felt about Elizabeth, or anyone, the way I feel about you. It tore me apart then, and it's tearing me apart now."

She opened her mouth, but no words would come. When his did, they clawed at that cold, scarred place deep inside her.

"I had to go, Meg. I couldn't keep using you. I loved you too much." He swallowed tightly. "I still love you. More than you'll ever know. That's why I'll go, if that's what you want. I'll leave you in peace, Meg. Just say the word."

Megan shifted to look at him. His eyes were closed, his jaw set, as if he was waiting for a death blow. In the pale light, she saw the glint of moisture in the thick fringe of his lashes, and the last remnants of that long-ago anger drained away.

There on the beach, in the silver glow of a California winter moon made hazy by the warm Santa Ana wind, Megan realized something she knew she should have understood long ago. Had she meant less to him six years ago, he could have easily kept up the charade, and hung on to her until he'd drained her of the strength he needed to keep going. He could have continued the deception, could have taken and taken and taken, making the break—when she finally discovered the truth—crippling, instead of merely agonizingly painful.

She thought of all the times she had wished she could hurt him back, had wished she could throw in his face all the harsh condemnation and reproach she felt, calling him every horrible thing she had thought him then. And only now did she realize that if he *had* been what she'd thought him, nothing she could have said, no epithets she could have hurled at him, would have bothered him at all.

And if he wasn't that kind of man, her words would have broken him.

He'd had no choice. At long last she saw it. He'd had to leave her, or break under the pressure. Just as she had once been his salvation, she had become his torture, the last straw that made the burden too much for him to bear.

"Oh, Dev," she whispered, and reached for him.

Eight

——

Dev grabbed her wrists, staring at her in shock.

"Meg?"

It came out husky, thick. For the first time, there in the moonlight on a deserted beach, he found Meggie looking out of Megan Spencer's clear blue eyes.

"I don't want you to go away," she whispered, sending a shiver of sensation racing down his spine. "I didn't understand, Dev. I do, now."

"If you're feeling sorry for me because of—"

"Stop. I've never felt sorry for you, Dev. I've hurt for you, even when all I knew was that you were in pain. I've ached for you, wishing you would let me help. And I've cried for you, and me, when I thought you weren't the man I believed you were."

She took a shaky breath. "But I see now that you had no choice. That you had to leave, because you *were* the kind of man I believed you were. And I see now that if you had been the kind of cheat I tried to convince myself you were afterward, that you would have stayed, because lying would have meant nothing to you.''

"God, Meg . . .''

"I still wish you'd told me . . . but I understand why you didn't.''

"But I hurt you so badly. . . .''

"Yes,'' she admitted. "But only because I didn't understand. I thought you'd left because you'd gotten all you wanted from me.''

Dev groaned, his hands slipping from her wrists to her fingers, holding them tightly. "I was afraid you'd think that,'' he whispered, "but I—''

"Shhh.'' Megan hushed him gently. "I know.''

"I really did try to find you,'' Dev said, his breath catching as she shifted her fingers, stroking her thumb over his hand. "As soon as it was . . . over.''

"I believe you.''

"I never stopped loving you, Meggie.'' He smothered a sigh as she moved her hands until they held his. "And there's never been anyone else, since you.''

Megan froze. "No one?''

"No one.''

She looked doubtful, and he gave her a rueful look. "Jeff didn't understand, either. He kept trying to get me to go out. One night a few years ago, we went out for pizza and a beer. He was trying to talk me into going out with this friend of his girlfriend's—his wife, now. Said two years was long enough to be moping around. Well, one beer turned into a few, and we both got pretty ripped. I don't remember it, but I guess he kept nagging at me about getting out, rejoining the world, finding a girl, and finally I told him to butt out, except I didn't word it quite so politely. At least, that's what he says.''

Megan smiled, a soft little smile that did crazy things to his insides. "Did he 'butt out'?"

"Yeah, he did. Which isn't like Jeff. One day I asked him why he'd taken no for an answer for the first time since I'd known him." He suppressed a shiver as she began to stroke his palm with her slender fingers. "He said he backed off because I told him that night that if I couldn't have Meggie, I didn't want anybody."

Megan gasped, her fingers stilling. Dev went on softly. "He never asked me who Meggie was, and he never mentioned that night until I brought it up myself that day."

She sighed, a long, low exhalation. Slowly she lifted his hands to her face, pressing them to her cheeks. Then she turned her head, first to one side, then the other, pressing a kiss in each of his palms.

"Meg," he said, a shudder rippling through him.

"Do you know what's scared me the most, for the last six years?"

Dev shivered again at the husky note in her voice. "What?" he managed to get out.

"The thought that you were the only one who could ever make me *feel*. Make me want. And that I'd lost you, forever."

"What about . . . ?"

He let the question trail off, unfinished. He didn't really want to know about her husband, anyway. He couldn't bear to think of her with another man, running to him while still wounded from his own betrayal. Besides, her soft admission was making it hard to think of anything except the heat it roused in him.

She leaned forward then and pressed her lips softly to his. Dev felt the heat begin to spiral out of control and yanked his mouth away.

"God, Meg, don't. Don't. I've spent every day of those six years wanting you. Don't torment me with what I can't have."

"Why can't you?"

His heart leapt at the soft, glowing admission of need that was lighting the blue eyes before him, even as he stared at her in disbelief.

"Meg? What . . ." He swallowed. "What do you want?"

"For the first time in so very long, I want to feel. I want to remember that night we had, Dev. I want to know that it was as incredible as I remember."

Shock rippled through him; he'd never expected this. Every nerve in his instantly aware body screamed its answer, but his mind was still reeling.

"Meg," he breathed, shaking his head.

"Don't ask any questions, please. I don't have any answers. Not tonight. Tomorrow will be here soon enough. Tonight I don't want to think. Or talk anymore. I just want to *feel,* Dev. Alive, like you used to make me feel. I haven't felt like that in so long. . . ."

He knew it was wrong, knew she was still too confused to be making this decision rationally, but when had rationality ever been a part of this? And in the deepest, darkest corner of his mind, there lurked the realization that this might be all he ever had of her, that when she reached her final decision, it might be the goodbye he dreaded. With the shaking hands of a man afraid that his perfect vision will shatter at the first touch, he reached for her.

Every bit of the longing of six years was poured into that first kiss, and Dev nearly melted under its force. Her mouth was warm and urgent, and when his lips parted hers he waited for the touch of her tongue with an eagerness that stunned him. When it came, hot and wet and fierce, and he heard her gasp at the pleasure of it, he echoed her cry with his own.

"Meggie," he said huskily as he at last broke the kiss. He raised his hands to her head, tugging at the twist of her hair. "Do you know I've never seen it down?"

He loosened some of the pins, and she gave a quick shake of her head, sending the honey-colored mass flying. He sucked in a breath as that sweet gardenia scent rose up to him; that breath caught in his throat as he stared at her.

"I loved the way it looked before, but this is..."

He didn't finish, but the way Meg let her head loll back, as if she liked the feel of his hands caressing the silken strands, told him she understood.

"We'd better stop," he said thickly, the hot, avid look in his eyes belying the words.

She slid her hands up to his neck, lacing her fingers at his nape. "Why?"

"Because," he ground out, "if we don't, we're never going to leave this beach."

"Do we need to leave this beach? It's warm... soft... private."

He let out a strangled exclamation. "Meg, stop."

She looked at him dreamily, then her eyes suddenly widened as her face paled. "I guess we're not... prepared for this, are we?"

"I'm prepared," he said flatly, remembering a time when he hadn't been, and hadn't given it a second thought. They'd been lucky once; he wasn't about to take chances again.

"Oh." It was a tiny little sound, and Dev realized what she was thinking.

"I didn't plan this, Meg. Jeff's about as subtle as Texas. He thinks stuffing a condom into my wallet every time he can get away with it will encourage me to 'rejoin the human race,' as he puts it."

Her expression cleared. "Then what...?"

"You deserve better than this," he said gruffly. "A quick fumble on the beach, without—"

"Who said anything about quick?" she whispered, and kissed him again.

Any hope he had of controlling the situation vanished in a flare of heat when she slid her hands up under his light cotton sweater to caress his chest. Her mouth was dancing, coaxing, her fingers slipping over his flesh and leaving fiery trails. In one swift movement he reached down and tugged the sweater over his head.

Megan lifted her head then, watching him as she slid her palms over him, stroking, until her fingers flicked over his nipples. His eyes closed, and he sucked in a quick, deep breath as the flat, brown discs puckered under her touch.

As if experimenting, she moved one hand tentatively down his chest to his belly, making a circular caress around his navel. He felt the deep muscles there ripple, contracting in a convulsive wave beneath her hand, and he groaned in reaction.

"It's still there between us, isn't it?" she asked, blue eyes touched with wonder as she looked up at him.

"It never went away," he said hoarsely, lifting his hand to the zipper of the bright blue jumpsuit she wore. Then he paused, his eyes asking the question. In answer, she kicked off her shoes and lifted her hands to cup his face.

"Make me feel alive again, Dev. I've held it in for so long."

His mouth came down on hers fiercely as he tugged at the zipper that slanted at an angle across the front of the jumpsuit. The soft blue fabric parted, and he pulled her close, desperate to feel the heat of her against him. He sucked in a breath when he finally felt the soft curves of her breasts searing his chest.

"Meg...Meggie..." The breath hissed out of him as she twisted sinuously, her nipples two points of fire against his skin through the flimsy lace of her bra. He gulped, and tried again. "You really want this?"

"I want you," she said simply.

The words sent a rocket of heat careening through him, bringing his already surging body to a hardness that was almost painful. He growled something he wasn't sure was even a word as he unfastened the bra, then swept the jumpsuit and the lacy blue panties down her legs and tossed them aside. She sagged against him, and he eased her back on the sand.

He was beyond thinking about champagne, candlelight, fine sheets and all the other things he would have wished for this night—all he knew was that Meggie, his Meggie, was back, she wanted him, and he wanted her so badly it was making his knees weak.

He just knelt there beside her, frozen, staring, his eyes drinking in the full, ripe swell of her breasts, the incredibly long, silken legs and the sweet, womanly curve of her hips, all painted in moonlight.

"Oh, Meggie, you're even more beautiful than I remembered," he whispered hoarsely.

He meant it. She'd been a girl then; she was all woman now, lusciously curved. She would cradle him so sweetly, her legs would—

Whoa, Cross, he cautioned himself, or this will be the shortest flight in history. Then she held her arms out to him in invitation, and he reached quickly to undo the buttons of his jeans.

His fingers were clumsy, or perhaps it was the strain on the fabric from his arousal, but it seemed to take forever. When his hands at last went to the waistband to tug them off, he saw her eyes fastened on him avidly. He stopped, an odd little shiver going through him.

"Do you mind?" Her voice was husky, hot somehow.

"When you sound like that," he said through teeth clenched against a wave of pure, searing pleasure, "I don't mind anything."

"I just want to look at you," she said shyly, as if she wasn't sure that was something she should want. "I didn't really get to before...."

Dev felt himself flush slightly, but stood and slid the jeans off his narrow hips, wincing a little at the tug of denim over his aching flesh. He felt her eyes on him, felt himself tighten even more, and when she said softly, "You're the beautiful one," he went down to her like melted butter.

She welcomed him, and he pressed the silken length of her to him hungrily. He kissed her, long and hard and deep, rocking his mouth over hers as his tongue delved again for the honeyed warmth he remembered so well. She twisted, her breasts pressing against his chest, and when he lowered his head to nuzzle them she cried out.

He cupped the soft weight of her in his hands, lifting the already taut peaks to his lips. He captured first one, then the other, flicking, tugging, until she was moaning and arching, offering herself for more of the luscious caresses.

He meant to make this special for her, wanted to erase any memory of that long-ago morning when he'd hurt her so badly. But she was touching him so sweetly, stroking him, her hands running over him as little sounds of discovery rose from her, and he knew he was unraveling much too quickly. But when he tried to draw away, she made a bereft little sound that drew him back as if on a string.

"Meg..." She moved again, finding another tingling bunch of nerves he hadn't known he had. "Ah, Meggie... We've got to slow down...wait..."

"I've been waiting. Too long."

Her breath was hot and eager against his ear, and he shuddered. And then he was kissing her, trailing his mouth over her, burning path after path of searing, aching heat, until she was writhing beneath him, begging him to come to her and end the torture. And when he could no longer stand it himself, he did, taking care of protecting her before settling his body over hers.

He felt her heat as his rigid flesh probed her softness, knew that he'd reached the point of no return. Although his body screamed at him, he knew he had to give her this last chance.

"Meggie . . . you're sure? Really sure?"

"Please," she begged. "I'm so empty. Fill me, Dev."

"I love you, Meggie," he said thickly, and he did as she'd asked, sliding himself into her welcoming body. "I love . . . Oh, Meg . . ."

He shuddered, every muscle going tense as he held himself still, fighting the need to plunge forward. Sweat beaded up on him, covering his body with a damp sheen as he tried to go slowly. She was so tight, so incredibly tight, that if he hadn't known it was impossible, he would swear she'd been with no one in years.

"Meggie . . ."

"Don't stop, I need you, Dev!"

She bucked suddenly beneath him, driving her hips upward and finishing what he'd begun. He was sheathed inside her, hard and full and deep, and her cry was one of mingled pain and pleasure. To resist her dancing, coaxing flesh now was impossible, and he began to move.

Megan watched him, saw the tight look of need on his face change to breathless pleasure as he took her higher and higher, felt his skin, satin over taut, flexing muscle, beneath her hands, and reveled in the wonderful fullness he brought to her as he filled her again and again. She felt the pressure building in her until she could barely breathe, until she thought each driving thrust, each sound that broke from him, would send her flying.

His hand crept between them, seeking, then finding her slick flesh. She gasped out as heat flared through her from beneath his hand, meeting and joining that already blazing from his hard, driving body. She cried out his name, over and over, heard him groan hers in return until, just as she heard him cry out hoarsely that he couldn't wait, her body convulsed, then erupted into a writhing, wild thing that was aware of nothing but the shattering of all her boundaries and the hot, fiery pulse of Dev within her.

"Meggie. Oh, Meggie..."

He panted it again and again, as little tremors rocked him, echoes of the most incredible explosion he'd ever known. He felt her arms tighten around him, remembered how her fingers had felt clutching at his back, and at the end, digging into his buttocks as she took him home for the last time, and another shudder rippled through him.

"Oh, Dev," Megan whispered, still quivering as he collapsed against her, his breath ragged against her skin. Tiny pulsing echoes of that fierce explosion rippled through her, and she knew she had her answer: it was, indeed, as incredible as she'd remembered.

It was a long time before he spoke. At last, in a voice that was soft with wonder, he said slowly, "Six years. Six years I spent telling myself I was crazy, that it couldn't really have been like this. That it was the circumstances, that I was building it up because I knew I couldn't have it anymore..."

"I know," she whispered, still holding him tight.

They lay in silence, there on the sand, the surf and the salt-tanged air their only company. The warm Santa Ana wind had died to a mere breeze, and the sand still held some of the day's warmth; it kept the night chill from them.

When he could move again, Dev gathered her gently into his arms once more, and held her close for a long time. When her hands began to move over him, gently, coaxingly, he made love to her again, so long and so sweetly that she was nearly hoarse from crying out her pleasure long before he took his own.

He could barely move then, and he stretched out beside her, pulling her into the curve of his body. Dev couldn't remember ever knowing a feeling so peaceful, so sweet, as having her curled up beside him, her soft breath feathering over his skin. He slept as he hadn't in years, deeply, tranquilly, feeling at long last as if he'd found his way home.

When he awoke with a start in the star-brightened darkness after the moon had set, his arm tightened convulsively around her as if he wasn't sure she was real. She responded with a fierce, urgent kiss that told him she'd been awake, waiting for him. The thought sent his blood pounding in heated, heavy beats, and by the time her slender hands slipped down his belly to caress him, he was a hot, satin-smooth weight against her fingers.

The next time they awoke, dawn was beginning to light the sky, and in a sudden flurry of shyness, Meg dressed hurriedly. Sand, they discovered, had a knack for working its way into every fold of cloth, not to mention some of the more tender areas of the body.

"Meg," Dev began, sensing her unease, "are you all right?"

"I need to go home," she said abruptly, fumbling with the zipper of her jumpsuit.

"I know. I'll take you. But are you all right?"

"Fine. I just have…a lot of things to do before the party tonight."

He'd forgotten about that. Completely. Not, he thought wryly as he dug his other shoe out of the sand, that anyone could blame him, all things considered. He'd brought her here last night with only the hope that she would listen, and perhaps understand. He'd never expected, never even dared to hope for such sweetness.

Still, they had spent the night making love on the beach like a couple of teenagers; he supposed Meg had a right to be embarrassed. Not to mention that she was going to have some explaining to do to the redoubtable Mrs. Moreland, he thought with an inward smile. He hoped her son was not an early riser—handling that might be a bit much for her, in her current state of mind.

Although, Dev thought as he watched her wrestle with her own shoes, it might be just as well for the boy to get used to him now. The sooner Kevin got accustomed to his presence, the better, because he wasn't about to let Meg slip through his fingers again.

They started up toward the Jeep, and Dev found himself smiling as he looked at the bulldozer that was sitting a few yards away. There wouldn't be any problem, he told himself. He and Kevin had gotten along fine yesterday. Of course, that was a lot different from getting along with the guy who wants to marry your mother.

Meg scrambled into the Jeep as if her life depended on moving quickly. Dev got in a little slower and turned to look at her before he started the motor.

"Meg, look, I know this wasn't exactly the most romantic night in the world. We should have gone somewhere else—"

"No. I-it was perfect." She colored at her own words, and shoved at the sandy tangle of her hair. "But I'm having a little trouble with the morning after."

Dev winced. "Are you...sorry?"

She stopped the jerky movements then, and looked at him. "No," she said at last, "I'm not sorry, Dev. But I need time to think."

Dev's jaw tightened. He didn't like the sound of that. He wanted her to feel as wonderful as he did, as certain that everything would work out. But perhaps the forgiveness that had come last night wasn't up to the glaring light of day.

"All right," he said at last, reluctantly. "Just remember one thing. I had no choice, once. But I won't give you up again."

He saw by her expression that she understood; if it *was* to end between them once and for all, it would be her doing. But there was something else haunting her eyes, something he didn't understand, some shadowy look of doubt that made him uneasy.

He didn't want to examine it now. He wanted to cling to the unbelievable sweetness of the night they'd shared, and believe in the miracle he'd been handed: Meggie, back in his arms and loving him.

He started the Jeep and put it in gear.

Megan stood on the porch, watching the black Jeep round the curve and disappear. She stood still, listening, until she couldn't hear it any longer.

I won't give you up again.

His words echoed in her ears, mocking her. With a tiny moan, she turned and ran into the house. It was quiet. Mrs. Moreland and Kevin were thankfully still asleep, and her father wasn't due back from Sacramento until this afternoon.

Moments later she stood in a steaming shower, washing the sand from her body and scrubbing her hair and scalp until it tingled. And she wasn't, she insisted, crying again; it was the shower.

Everything had seemed so simple last night. Dev had told her everything he should have told her long ago, and she had understood at last why he'd had no choice but to leave her.

She could, she thought, forgive him for that. If she thought long and hard about the pressure he'd been under, she could even forgive him for not telling her about being married. And ironically, things had become so turned around that what had devastated her so then, his leaving, had now become the very proof that she hadn't been wrong about him at all.

And that should have resolved things. That and the sweetest night she'd ever known, a night of heated caresses and loving touches, a night of soaring flights and unbelievable pleasure. A night that had proven to her once and for all that Devlin Cross was the one man with the power to make her sing, body and soul and heart.

Yet it hadn't; it had only complicated matters further. Again she had horrible choices to make. Could she trust Dev with the truth about Kevin? Or would the revelation of her own lie destroy them just as his had six years ago?

She stepped out of the shower and reached for a towel, scrubbing her body until long after the water was gone. She needed the sensation of near pain to distract her from the new dilemma she found herself in. For now, in the light of day, far removed from the hot, fiery pleasures of the night, the question wasn't whether she could forgive Dev, it was whether *he* could forgive *her*.

Nine

Dev paused in the doorway of the trailer when he saw Frank Mason digging through the stack of papers on the desk with sharp, irritated movements. With a sigh he braced himself. It seemed every encounter with the man lately was an angry one, and he was in no mood today. He'd been given a taste of paradise, and now had to just sit and wait to find out if a taste was all he was ever going to have.

Mason straightened and whirled as if startled. For a moment he just gaped at Dev, whose brow furrowed at the man's reaction. Then Mason recovered, and was shouting before Dev even got through the door.

"Damn it, what is this? Jackson says you told him we're going to have to use trench jacks for the damn storm drain!"

So much for the heat of a Santa Ana wind as an excuse for the man's temper, Dev thought. The winds had died out early this morning—when he was taking Meg home, he thought with a pang—and Mason was still raving.

"Only for fifty yards or so," he clarified, trying to speak calmly as he crossed to the desk.

"Only? It might as well be a mile! And we purposely changed the depth so we wouldn't have to do that! We even cut the size of the pipe to the minimum to save more time!"

"But you're still going to have to cut through that knoll, and the soil there is too sandy to go that deep without them."

"Do you know how much that's going to cost? Not to mention how long it might take. There's a lot of construction going on now—it might take days to get trench jacks out here if they're all tied up elsewhere! Weather reports say a storm's on its way, and by then it might be pouring rain, and we'll have to shut down altogether!"

Dev sat down behind the desk, waiting until at last the man had to pause to take a breath. "Yes. But there's no choice. Without trench jacks to stabilize the drain, you could have a cave-in."

"Hell!" Mason snorted. "What are the chances of that in a measly fifty yards, when it'll only be open for one day, maybe two?"

Dev restrained himself from pointing out that a moment ago, that fifty yards had been a mile. He thought of Harlan Spencer's words: "Whatever version of the truth is going to get the results he wants." The senator, it seemed, knew his man.

"Any chance is too high," Dev said, "when you've got men working at risk."

"Save me the holier-than-thou crap," Mason snapped. "You know, Cross," he said, slamming his fist on the desk, "if I wasn't sure you weren't getting anything out of it, I'd swear you were sabotaging this project."

Dev's head came up sharply, his eyes going utterly cold. Slowly he got to his feet, and without a word he began to gather up the papers scattered across the desk.

"All right, all right, take it easy. I said I was sure you weren't getting anything out of it."

Dev moved the phone, setting it out of the way, then picked up the stack of papers it had been holding down and added them to the others.

"Damn, you're a stubborn— Put that stuff down."

Dev put the phone neatly back on the bare spot.

"Will you listen to me?"

Dev pulled open a desk drawer, grabbed a couple of file folders and slid them into the battered canvas bag that served as a briefcase.

"Come on, Dev, I know you need this job. And I know how bad."

Dev's head came up again. "There was a time," he said coldly, "when you would have been right. I would have needed this job badly enough to stomach even that."

But there's nothing left that's worth that much to me anymore, he finished inwardly. Except the one thing I may still lose.

Mason ran a hand over his hair distractedly, then patted the empty pocket that usually held at least two of the fat cigars. "Look, Dev," he said, "I've got investors breathing down my neck, and I'm having a hard time stalling them off. Every day we fall behind it gets worse."

Dev merely looked at him.

"You know damn well it's too late for me to change geologists now! By the time I get a new man in and set up, I'll be more behind than ever!"

"*I* know that. I just wasn't sure you did."

Mason stared at him. "Why, you—" He stopped, sputtering. "Damn, what do you want—an apology? All right, I'm sorry. Satisfied?"

"No. But it's a start."

Mason managed a coaxing smile. "Look, son, I know I'm about as subtle as a tank, but I really do have a lot of people on my back. And I know if you'd been a straight nine-to-five man, we wouldn't even be this far along. So forget it, will you?"

Dev hesitated. He'd had about enough of Mason running hot and cold, but the man was right about one thing. Dev did need the job.

"All right," he said reluctantly, at last.

"Good." Unfortunately Mason found and lit one of his noxious cigars, and puffed on it expansively. "Tell you what. Why don't you get out of here? Take the day off, and the weekend. Haven't had a whole weekend off since you started this job." He looked extremely pleased with himself. "Don't want to see you set foot out here until Monday."

"I thought you wanted—"

"You think too much."

Now those, Dev thought wryly, were probably the truest words the man had ever spoken.

"I was going to start on the new slope—" he began.

"We won't even be ready to start grading for the park until the end of next week." Mason's expression changed, tightened. "Damn, never had so much trouble getting a man to take some time off. What is it with you?"

Dev could have told him that he preferred the distraction of work to the painful directions in which "too much thinking" might take him, but he was too busy trying to reconcile this man, who was trying to get him to slow down, with the man who, moments ago, had been accusing him of being behind all the delays the project had encountered.

"What's with you?" Dev countered. "Aren't you the guy who's been pushing for light-speed around here?"

The look that flashed across Mason's face was peculiar, reminding Dev of a child sneaking out of a store with a stolen candy bar in his pocket. Then it was gone, his gruffly jovial demeanor back in place.

"Hey, let's just say I owe you after that smart remark I made. Get out of here, and I'll see you tonight at the senator's party."

Mason was gone before Dev could voice any more protests. The party tonight, he thought. The party that Meg had been trapped into inviting him to. The party he now had no idea if she would welcome him to or not.

But he was going anyway, he thought in sudden determination. He knew she wasn't sure yet how she felt, even after the incredible night they'd spent. But he knew as well that they struck sparks every time they were together, and he wasn't above using that to his advantage, not when whatever chance he had with her was at stake.

He felt a sense of relief as he left the site and drove to the shop where he'd rented a tuxedo for the elaborate birthday party. He was through with self-recriminations, he decided. He couldn't change what had happened; he'd explained as best he could, and it was up to her now.

With a wry smile at the incongruity of the sight, he hung the formal suit from the Jeep's roll bar. The thought occurred to him that Meg might not want to talk to him at all. She'd asked for time, and he'd promised it to her. And in the kind of crush he knew this party was going to be, she wouldn't have any trouble avoiding him if that was what she wanted. Except that he was determined to have this last chance, and he wasn't about to let anything stop him.

He spent the rest of the day catching up on everything in the new office. It wasn't a day off, as Mason had ordered, but he found just waiting nearly impossible, and needed the distraction. He had remembered the papers he'd carried away from the trailer, and was reaching for the canvas bag when the phone rang. He grabbed for it, hoping it might be Meg, and had to slow his racing pulse when he heard Jeff Russell's lazy drawl.

Jeff assured him everything was under control, that he was just checking in, since Dev hadn't called in a while.

"Sorry," he muttered.

"It's okay. How are things going there? You sound a little at loose ends."

"I am, at the moment. It's weird. Mason's been pushing like a bulldozer for weeks, and now all of a sudden he's got all the time in the world. Told me to take the rest of the day off *and* the weekend."

"Well, hallelujah for the man then, if he got you to take time off. Naturally, you're at the office, right?"

"What's that supposed to mean?"

"Just that I know what your idea of a day off is. You don't know how to relax, buddy."

"I could learn."

It slipped out as he thought of the morning he would have gladly spent doing nothing more than holding Meg, making sweet, long love to her for hours. They were going to have that morning, he thought suddenly, fiercely. And a whole lot more mornings. And afternoons. And nights...

"Dev? You okay?"

"Yeah." He sounded a little too fervent, his voice echoing with the determination he was feeling. He toned it down. "I'm fine."

After he'd hung up, he wondered what Jeff would say if he told him he'd found Meg again. After all this time, after all these years.... Jeff would understand. Jeff alone knew about the woman who'd haunted him all these years.

Well, she wasn't going to haunt him any longer, Dev thought, sitting up to sort through the papers in the canvas bag. She was going to be a part of his life in reality, he'd make sure of that. And he refused to even entertain the thought that whatever doubts were still plaguing Meg might make it impossible for her to forgive and forget. He

couldn't, he *wouldn't* let that happen. He'd lost her once—
he wasn't about to lose her again.

He was expecting a lot of her, he realized. To ask her to
forget—

He stopped, his thoughts derailed by the paper in his
hands. It had been caught behind another sheet, snagged on
a staple, and he wondered for a moment if it was what Mason had been looking for when he'd been digging through
the pile on the desk.

It must be for another job, Dev thought as he looked at
the packing slip for steel rivets. This couldn't be for the Gold
Coast project, even if that's what it said, because the rivets
were number five, not the stronger number eights called for
in the designs.

Or it must be for a different part of the project than the
plans he'd seen, Dev decided. He was a geologist, not an
architect. But he'd picked up a lot on all the various projects he'd worked on, and he didn't remember anything in the
design of this one that didn't call for the stronger rivets. And
he knew, as well, that once the riveting was done, and both
ends of the installed rivet rounded off, it would be virtually
impossible to tell the difference between fives and eights.
Except, he thought grimly, in the reduced strength of the
entire structure.

Dev shook his head sharply. It had to be a mistake. He'd
ask Mason about it on Monday, he thought, replacing the
packing slip in the bag. He reached for the other papers,
then stopped, his hand suspended over them as an image of
a conversation he'd overheard played back in his head like
a video tape.

"Funny," one of the concrete workers had been saying to
another, "I would have figured they'd use twelve-inch centers for the reinforcement for this kind of thing." The man
had gestured to the layout of reinforcing steel rebar they'd

been standing next to. "But I'd swear this is spaced at fourteen."

Had the plans called for rebar every twelve inches? Had Mason extended it to fourteen inches? It would save—Dev scribbled some numbers quickly—one shaft of the expensive steel for every three feet. That could pile up on a project this size.

Another memory shot to the surface, of Mason grabbing a scribbled note out of his hand. He remembered the only word he'd been able to decipher had looked like *flyash*.

He'd thought nothing of it at the time, but now the word hovered over him like some malevolent shadow. The burnt residue, the unburnable ash that was the bane of air-quality people anywhere near plants that produced it, was often used by unscrupulous manufacturers; substituting the ash for part of the cement produced concrete that was cheaper... and also weaker.

Dev shook his head, thinking his imagination was really getting out of hand. But what if that note had been something other than just an idle scribble of a funny word that would be familiar to a developer like Mason? What if he'd been considering using it? What if he already had?

He tried to look at it reasonably. He was taking wild guesses, jumping to conclusions that might not be the right ones at all. There was probably an explanation for all of this.

But what if the crazy idea was true? What about all that talk about his investors? Was Mason in so much trouble that he would cut corners this badly? True, any one of these things alone probably wouldn't endanger the project, but all of them together? And what if there were more? If he's cut corners here, he's probably cut them elsewhere, Dev thought. And a combination of a lot of cut corners could be a formula for disaster. A real—

That thought came to an abrupt halt as another rose in its place, making his stomach knot until he thought he was going to be sick. Dear God, if it was true . . . what if Meg's father knew? He and Mason were old buddies, and had been in constant contact throughout this project. The senator had been to the site, and he himself had heard Mason more than once pleading for the senator's help in controlling his investors.

It couldn't be, he thought. He just couldn't reconcile the idea with what he knew and had seen of the senator. And no one had a more sterling reputation than Harlan Spencer. But then again, he also had a reputation for being loyal to his friends.

God, it couldn't be. It would just kill Meg. I can't deal with this, Dev thought suddenly. All I care about right now is Meg. All I—

He cut off his own thoughts abruptly. *I can't deal with this.* Just like he hadn't been able to deal with telling Meg the truth six years ago. Just like he hadn't been able to deal with facing her pain. Just like he hadn't been able to deal with the thought that he might have left her pregnant.

You're a damned coward, Cross, he told himself acidly. Admit it. And for once in your life, do something about it.

He would, he thought determinedly. Tonight.

Megan studied her reflection critically in the mirror, then picked up a tissue and blotted her lips once more. Satisfied, she nodded and exchanged a few words with the two other women in the country club's ladies' room, then turned to start back to the large, crowded banquet room. And every step of the way she told herself she wasn't going to spend one minute searching the throng of her father's friends and supporters for one particular tall, lean figure.

But she couldn't help the little twinge that rippled through her. What if he'd decided not to come? She'd asked for time to think—what if he thought she'd meant she didn't want him here?

She paused to take a steadying breath just outside the door, smoothing the dark, midnight blue of her dress. The rich velvet was cut in flowing lines from the deep V-neck front and back down to a full, sweeping skirt that brushed the top of her silk pumps. The color was so deep, so dark, that it almost appeared black, until she moved and the light caught the lustrous sheen of the blue as the fabric rippled over her slender body.

The single strand of pearls at her throat was her only ornament, and the only adornment the striking dress needed. With the memory in her mind of his look when she'd shaken her hair free on the beach, she'd worn it loose tonight, brushed to a silken sheen and falling in soft waves to her shoulders. She had, she admitted, dressed with extra care tonight. She hoped it wouldn't be for nothing.

She walked into the ballroom, and almost instantly her eyes zeroed in on a tall, lean figure near the outer doors, his back toward her. She told herself she was being foolish, that it could be anyone, but she knew it wasn't true. Only one man made her pulse leap like this. Only one man made her breath catch so suddenly in her throat that it nearly made her dizzy.

When she could move, she started across the room, intent on her goal. But her progress was impeded by everyone, it seemed, all wanting to comment on the success of the party. She felt like a fish swimming upstream as she battled her way forward.

Then he turned, and she stopped dead. God, she thought, stunned, he truly is beautiful. She'd never seen him in a tux, never known he could look so utterly right in the formal clothing, so striking in the traditional classic black. And she had never known he could look so imposing, so intimidating.

Only then did she notice the other looks he was getting, curious glances and outright stares—mostly from women, she noted, feeling an odd tightness in her chest.

Her father—she hadn't even noticed him standing there, she realized in shock—had his hand on Dev's arm and was drawing him aside. Harlan, looking distinguished in the gray tuxedo Megan had ordered him to wear as the guest of honor, was smiling broadly. But after a few moments, his expression became serious. Megan moved forward, unable to help herself, she had to hear what they were talking about.

"I don't mean to take advantage of your friendship with Mr. Mason," Dev was saying. "I know how close you are."

"We've known each other for many years. But what is it you're getting at ?"

Dev hesitated, then let out a breath. "Is he... Do you know if he's in any kind of financial trouble?"

"Frank?" Harlan seemed surprised at the idea. "Not that I know of. Why do you ask?"

"He's pushing awfully hard on this project."

"He always was a go-getter."

"So I gathered. But this..." Dev shrugged again. "He says his investors are on the prowl, putting pressure on him."

"Investors have that tendency," Harlan said reasonably.

"Especially if they're going by his original time line."

"Oh?"

"I've seen it. I'm no contractor, but it looks impossible to me."

"Because of delays?"

"Partly. But..." He hesitated, then plunged ahead. "I'm not sure it wasn't from the start."

Harlan's brows lowered. "That's a touchy thing to say."

"I know, sir." He sighed. "And I'm not sure of anything. But a few odd things have come up."

"Like what?"

"I think he's cutting corners. A lot of them."

"Now, wait a minute, son. Frank may be a little rough around the edges, but—"

"He's using cheaper materials. Maybe even cheating on the original plans. He's—"

"I think you'd better slow down, Dev," Harlan warned. "Frank's an old friend."

"That's what I'm afraid of."

Harlan stiffened, and Dev regretted the words. He hadn't meant to let it slip out, that fear he'd tried to bury that somehow Meg's father was involved in this with his old friend, but it was too late now. Much too late, he realized, as Megan's startled gasp turned them both around. She'd heard it all; Dev knew that the minute he looked at her face. She was staring at him, shock mixing with a rising anger in her eyes.

"Just what are you insinuating, *Mr.* Cross? That Frank Mason is a crook? And that—" her voice started to rise "—*my father* is in on it?"

"Meg, I—"

"My name is Megan!" she snapped. "How dare you come here, on my father's birthday, and make such ridiculous accusations!"

"Megan, honey," Harlan began soothingly, then looked at Dev. "I know nothing about any of this, Dev. I promise you that. But if there's any truth to it, I'll—"

"Don't bother, Daddy," Megan said hotly, glaring at Dev. "He's not much on truth, anyway. If he was, he'd know better than to even think you could be involved in anything like that. If he was, he never would have even thought to accuse you of such dealings. If he was—" She stopped, choking back a sob. "If he was, he'd have told me the truth six years ago."

"Meg," Dev said, his voice low and harsh.

"Six years ago?" Harlan asked, his eyes narrowing.

"Just get out, Dev," Megan ordered. "I won't have you here among my father's friends, spreading lies about the one man who stood by me no matter what. He was there when I needed him, not you. He never abandoned me—"

"Abandoned you?" Harlan jerked around to face Dev. "It was you? Was it, damn it? Are you the one who seduced an innocent child and then walked out on her when she got pregnant?"

Dev nearly reeled backward from the verbal attack. He sucked in a breath, his eyes going to Meg's pale face, her eyes wide as she covered her mouth with one slender hand, as if to stop the words that had already escaped. The truth was there in her eyes, in every line of her trembling body.

"My God," he whispered.

With a tiny cry, Megan whirled and ran. Dev tried to move, to go after her, but he was too stunned to move. She hadn't gone to another man. She had already been pregnant when he'd left her. She'd borne his child. Alone. My God, he thought numbly. Kevin was his.

Megan sat in the big leather chair in the country-club office. Her arms were wrapped around herself, as if that could stop the shudders that rippled through her every few seconds.

Was this how Dev had felt? she wondered. Ashamed of running away, yet unable to face her, as she felt unable to face him? Knowing he'd lied to her, yet not knowing what else to do?

It had been a long time since she had really analyzed her motivations. She'd told herself she knew why she did what she did, but now she wondered if perhaps she hadn't been afraid of looking too closely, afraid that she might, deep down, find that little fool she had once been. She felt as if she were on the edge of a yawning cavern, and if she didn't

step carefully, if she didn't look at exactly what she was doing, she would plummet downward and be lost forever.

She knew now why Dev had lied; why had *she?* Had it
really been, as she'd told herself, to protect Kevin, to keep
him from being hurt in case the father he'd never known
didn't want him? Was it because she felt he had no right to
know, no right to the son whose existence he'd never considered? Or was it just to hurt him as she had been hurt, to
make him think she had replaced him so easily?

She'd been so angry with him, angrier than she'd ever
been with anyone, except perhaps her mother when she had
died. She remembered wailing to her father, refusing even
to allow him his own grief, insisting that if her mother had
loved her, she never would have left her.

And at last she realized, huddled there in the chilly office, that she truly hadn't let go of the last of her anger at
Dev. She understood why he'd done what he'd done, had
even acknowledged that he'd had no choice. But she hadn't
truly forgiven him for deserting her, just as, underneath it
all, she had never really forgiven her mother.

An image came to her then, of her father holding her on
his lap as if she were five instead of a determinedly "nearly
grown-up" fifteen, trying to explain that sometimes leaving had nothing to do with not loving someone.

And maybe, she thought now, with the feeling of having
arrived at the end of a long, hard journey, maybe sometimes it has everything to do with *loving* someone.

After a hurried swipe at her still-damp eyes, Megan ti-
died herself and prepared to return to the party. She had responsibilities here, she was the hostess, after all. At least
that's what she told herself. But she didn't believe it. She
knew what her real reason was. She had to find Dev. She had
to explain, make him understand.

She went back to the main room. She searched the crowd,
but found no sign of him. She avoided her father, although

she knew he'd seen her. She smiled at friends and the rest of the guests. She went through the motions of supervising the highly efficient staff that didn't need supervision at all. She organized the group to gather around as her father opened the many gifts that had been brought, despite her urging to the contrary. And finally, she had to face the truth. Dev was gone. And he wasn't coming back.

"Thank you, baby. It was a wonderful party."

"You're welcome, Dad."

Her response was automatic, as all her actions had been since she'd realized that Dev wasn't coming back. They carried the last of the presents into the library and set them on the desk.

"We'll deal with those tomorrow," he said, eyeing her pale face. "You look exhausted."

"I am a little tired."

"I just want to get this one..." He rooted around in the boxes until he found what he wanted. He held it up, a beautiful pewter sculpture of an eagle, caught and frozen in midair, looking as if at any second it would wheel and once again go soaring upward.

"It's wonderful, isn't it?"

"Yes," she whispered, her throat tight as she stared at Dev's gift. Long ago she had told him of her father's passion for the powerful bird that was the symbol of America. That he had remembered, and had cared enough to search out this perfect and obviously expensive piece, wrenched at emotions already raw.

"He didn't really believe I was involved, you know. He was just afraid because of what it would have done to you."

He held out the card that had accompanied the sculpture. Megan read it softly, barely aware she was saying the words aloud.

"'To the only politician in this country that I'm sure is as honest as its symbol. Happy Birthday, Senator. Devlin Cross.'"

Her voice broke on his name, and she nearly crushed the card in her suddenly fierce grip. Harlan came to her side, slipping an arm around her.

"He told me, honey. The whole story. What an awful mess."

Megan lifted her head to look at her father. "Don't hate him, Daddy. He ... It was so horrible for him."

"I know. If Catherine had gone like that ..." He shook his head. "I don't know what I would have done. But I don't hate him, Megan. Not now. Besides, I'm afraid he hates himself more than enough for the both of us. He was rather hard on himself. He left the party right after we spoke, looking as if he were in a state of shock." He hugged her tightly. "You'd better get some rest, baby. There are things I'd like to know, but we'll talk about it in the morning."

Megan hugged him fiercely. "I love you, Daddy. Thank you for always being there."

She lay awake long into the night, staring into the darkness, trying not to think of the previous evening, when that darkness had been spangled with stars and painted with moonlight. She couldn't help wondering if she'd lost everything all over again, thrown it away for good this time, with her own hands.

It seemed that she had just drifted off when a gentle shaking awakened her. She turned over, still groggy with sleep.

"Megan, wake up, honey."

"Dad?" She sat up. It was barely light out, but she could see his expression. "What's wrong?"

"I didn't want to wake you," he said in a voice so full of concern that it sent a shiver through her. "But I'm afraid one part of our talk can't wait."

"Dad—"

"I know now why you've been different around Dev. I know why you've changed so much since he's been here. But there's one thing I don't know." He paused, then asked with infinite gentleness, "Do you still love him, baby?"

She bit her lip, choking back a sob. "I . . . I don't know. I care, even though I don't want to. . . . It hurt so much—"

Harlan sighed. "I know, honey. And you don't have to explain your feelings to me. I hope that, even though I'm your father and I love you to distraction, I have enough sense not to interfere in something like this. But if you still care for him there's something you need to know."

"I . . . What?"

"I just got a phone call. There was an accident at the site." He saw her jerk, and grabbed her hand. "A man was killed. Dev is in the hospital. I don't know how bad he is."

Any doubts she'd had, any confusion, was seared away in one blazing instant of fear. Faced with the bleak hollowness of a world without him, Megan's last barriers crumbled. She loved Devlin Cross with all her heart, and she would never, ever, forgive herself if the knowledge had come too late.

"Oh, God," she moaned.

The tiny sound, muffled by her fist clenched against her lips, had barely faded away before she was on her feet and moving.

Ten

"**W**hat do you mean, he's not here?"

Megan's voice echoed with an odd combination of relief and dismay. Dev was alive, but he was gone.

"I'm sorry. He *was* here, but—"

"You said he had a concussion and cracked ribs—"

"Yes," the young nurse said, beginning to look a little harried. "A minor concussion. We tried to change his mind, but he was adamant about leaving."

"Surely he shouldn't be up walking around with a head injury," Megan exclaimed.

"No, he shouldn't," the young nurse said with a cynical tone that belied her age, "but you just can't tell some people what to do, even if it's for their own good."

"I doubt if he'd ever think being in a hospital was for his own good," Megan said grimly, then turned to her father. "We've got to find him. What if he tries to drive that damned Jeep and gets dizzy or something?"

"I know, honey," Harlan said. He looked at the nurse. "Did he talk to anyone? Say where he was so bound and determined to go?"

"No. Just that he had to get out of here." She hesitated. "He seemed rather distraught. Of course, seeing someone die, especially like that, is very upsetting."

"You don't know the half of it," Megan whispered in distress. "He's been there before."

"We'll find him, Megan. Do you know his phone number?"

She shook her head. "Not the one for his apartment. The office is in the book."

She didn't explain that she'd looked it up the morning after he'd walked into her life again, unable to believe that it had been there at her fingertips all along, and she hadn't known somehow.

"You call the office, then," he said, digging out his phone credit card. "I'll see what I can do about finding his home number."

Moments later, she hung up on the uselessly ringing connection and turned to look at her father. He had hung up the pay phone located beside hers, and was dialing again.

"Frank's office had his home number," he explained, but moments later he was shaking his head. "No answer."

Megan bit her lip, trying to think. After a moment her father reached for the phone again.

"Have there been any messages, Mrs. Moreland?"

Megan stared at him in surprise; it had never occurred to her that Dev might try to contact her. He must have truly convinced her father of his feelings.

"I don't suppose Dev Cross has shown up at the house, has he?" He paused, listening. "Well, it was worth a try. If you should hear from him, page me right away, will you?" He hung up and looked at Megan.

"The job site," she said suddenly. "Maybe he went back."

Harlan nodded and quickly dialed once more. Almost immediately he hung up, and Megan stared at him.

"Busy," he said succinctly.

"Then that's got to be it." She turned to go, barely restraining herself from breaking into a run.

"I think I'd better drive," Harlan said when they reached the car. "We barely made it here alive."

Megan didn't waste time arguing, but ran around to the passenger side of the sedan and got in. "Just hurry," she pleaded.

Even though her father did just that, it seemed to take forever to cover the few miles out to the construction site. She was so anxious that when her father slowed the car just before the gate, she didn't realize why until she saw him staring at something beyond the fence.

"Lord," he exclaimed.

Megan followed his gaze, and saw, atop a small knoll in the distance, a huge cement mixer lying on its side at an ungainly angle, half in a trench that was at least six feet deep. With its wheels pointed at an angle toward the sky, it looked like some kind of prehistoric beast that had fallen where it had been fatally wounded.

A low sound escaped from Megan, a whimper of pain and fear. She suppressed it with her fist to her lips, pressing the soft flesh against her teeth until it hurt.

When Harlan pulled off the road onto the construction site itself, they were stopped immediately by a man standing in front of a barrier made of yellow plastic tape strung between the chain-link fence posts. She'd seen that tape before, Megan thought suddenly, on the news, at the scene of some death or other horrible event. It hit her with a thud that this is what this place was now, a place where a man had died. And she felt a little spurt of guilt at her gratitude that it hadn't been Dev.

"Sorry," the man was saying. "Nobody beyond this point."

"We're here about the accident last night," Harlan said.

"Sorry. We're still investigating. That whole area is blocked off."

Megan noticed now that the man's hard hat was labeled Cal-OSHA. She knew from her work with her father that the state Occupational Safety and Health Administration investigated all industrial or job-related accidents. And that they could be very sticky about their investigations. Although she despised using her father's position for special treatment, all rules were off when it came to Dev, and she opened her mouth to plead with him to do what he so rarely did: pull rank. But before she could get the words out, Harlan spoke again, pulling out his identification.

"I'm Harlan Spencer, state senator for this district. I have a personal interest in this incident. A friend of mine was injured."

The man's brows rose. "He the guy who tried to pull the pipe mortar man out?"

"I don't know. Is that what happened?"

The man looked hesitant. "They haven't released the details yet."

"I'll have full access to the reports later," Harlan reminded him. "Please save us all some time and red tape. What on earth happened here?"

"Earth, exactly," the man said grimly, apparently decided now. "The edge collapsed. That trench was well over the four-foot minimum, but it's not shored at all. They didn't even use trench jacks."

"Use what?"

"Reinforcement plates with an adjustable jack in between them. You put them in open trenches and they brace the sides so that—'' he gestured at the fallen truck ''—doesn't happen.''

''I see,'' Harlan said grimly.

''Anyway,'' the man went on, pushing the yellow hard hat back from his forehead, ''guy was down in the hole, joining the drain pipe, when the mixer pulled up. The edge gave out, but not so bad then, from what the witnesses say. Truck just tilted a little. Everybody got out except one guy who was stuck between the truck and the pipe. The pipe held at first, so he wasn't hurt, just trapped. The geologist—that your friend?''

Harlan nodded.

''Gutsy guy. He was in there trying to get him out when the rest caved in and the truck went over. Damned lucky it didn't crush him, too.''

Megan smothered a tiny cry. Her father's expression grew even harder.

''Why didn't they call for help? The fire department or something?''

''They did,'' the man said with a disgusted snort. ''Eventually. But since there were no injuries in the beginning, they called the developer first—Mason, I think his name is. His orders, from what I hear. By the time he finally let them call the fire department, it was too late for the guy in the trench. All they could do was pull your buddy out.''

''Is he here?'' It was the first thing Megan had said, her voice low and tight.

''Your friend? They took him to the hospital. He was pretty banged up, but they said he'd be all right.''

''He checked out,'' Harlan told the man.

''Maybe he's at the trailer,'' Megan said, looking toward the long, white shape about as far out as the upended mixer but in the other direction.

"Could be," the man said. "He could have come in before I got here this morning. They just stuck me out here on the gate a while ago, so I don't know who came through before that. I don't know if I can let you through, though," he added regretfully.

"This project includes a state park," Harlan said, using the forceful tone that won him full attention on the senate floor. "That puts the investigation of this incident under my jurisdiction. Who's in charge?"

Megan had no idea if that was true, but the other man was convinced.

"Mr. Harding," he said. "He's over near the scene."

He stepped aside then, allowing them to pass. Harlan wheeled the sedan over the rutted road with much less care than it deserved. They neared the trailer, and Megan breathed a sigh of relief at the sight of the battered black Jeep.

"He's here."

"So is Frank," Harlan said, looking at the Mercedes.

"Yes," she said, her brow creasing. They walked toward the trailer, and the moment they rounded the corner they heard the voices.

"—that important to you?" Dev was saying incredulously. "A man died out there, damn it!"

"It was an accident—"

"Accident, hell! I told you you couldn't do that section without trench jacks, that it wouldn't take much to make it go without them. But you go ahead, don't even shore it up, and then drive a damned sixty-thousand-pound mixer up to the edge. In sandy loam, no less, where one good stamp of your feet can start a slide!"

"Your damned requirements put us weeks behind. It was a chance I had to take!"

"Except," Dev's voice came through clearly, "you didn't take the chance. Somebody else did, and now he's dead."

His voice went icy. "I was there, Mason. I heard his bones snap, heard him scream, and all I could do was hold his hand while he died."

Mason was silent, apparently affected by the grim description, but recovered quickly. "He knew the risk. And he was getting paid damn well for taking it!"

"Tell that to his widow, damn you. And his kids." Dev's voice dropped. "God, I've had enough of being helpless, watching people die."

"Look, Cross—"

"No wonder you wanted me out of here yesterday. You knew I'd blow the whistle on you. If I hadn't driven by after I left the party and seen what you were up to last night—"

"You're in this as deep as I am, Cross."

"Not a chance. I told you what you had to do to make it safe. If you chose to ignore it, and the law, it's your responsibility. Including," he said coldly, "that man's death."

Megan and her father got up the stairs to the door just in time to see a sly, furtive look come over Mason's face. "Well, now, what if I don't remember you telling me a thing about reinforcing that section of trench? If my geologist made a mistake, it's not my fault, now is it?"

Megan went rigid, and started to move forward, but her father held her back just outside the doorway. After a quick shake of his head, he turned his attention back to the men in the trailer, and she realized he wanted to listen to as much as possible before they were noticed.

With an effort, Megan stayed still. It was difficult for her, because Dev looked horrible. He wore the tuxedo pants and shirt, and she remembered what he'd said about driving by the site after the party. The shirt was smeared with dirt and blood, and she realized he must have come straight from the hospital, putting on the clothes he'd arrived in. He was pale beneath his tan, and she could see the tightness of his jaw, set against the pain. He had one hand braced on the high table in the corner, where the phone lay off the hook. His other arm was held tightly across his middle as if that could ease the ache of cracked ribs. There was a bandage at his temple, and an ugly bruise on his cheekbone on the same side.

"I gave you," Dev was saying carefully, "written reports on every foot of this project. Including the storm drain. And the need for trench jacks going through that knoll."

"Funny, I never saw anything about trench jacks."

For a split second Mason's eyes flicked to the briefcase he held. Dev looked puzzled, as if he were having difficulty understanding, then he shook his head as if he could shake off the effects of his injury and start thinking clearly again. He winced, his hand tightened on the edge of the table. Megan tensed as if to go to him, but again her father held her back. And after a moment, Dev steadied himself.

"So that's it," he said tightly. "That's why you were here even before I got here. You pulled my copies of the reports, didn't you?"

"What reports?"

"You bastard—"

"This project is worth millions, Cross. More than a two-bit operation like yours ever dreamed of. I'm not about to let it go down the tubes."

"So you sell me out instead."

"It might be worth something to you."

Dev swore again, sharply.

"Look, I know you need the money. Still paying off all those bills for your wife, aren't you?"

Dev jerked sharply, a short, compressed breath escaping him as the movement tugged at his ribs. He stared at Mason.

"Of course I know about it," Mason said. "I always know everything about the people I hire. I knew how deep a hole you were in. Why do you think I chose you in the first place? I knew you couldn't afford to be picky." He snorted. "Never figured you'd be a damned Boy Scout."

"Damn you."

"I'll give you one last chance, Cross. I'll make it worth your while to take the heat for this."

"Go to hell," Dev spat.

Mason shrugged. "Your loss. Don't forget, I have some very influential friends. Without these reports, you won't have a prayer."

It was the last straw for Megan—she couldn't stop herself from stepping into the trailer. Harlan had apparently heard enough, too, because he let her go. Dev spotted her instantly.

"Meggie . . ." he whispered.

Mason glanced over his shoulder at her, but missed seeing her father, still in the shadow of the doorway. "What the hell are you doing here?" he snapped at her.

"Shut up, Mason," Dev said before Megan could answer.

Mason whirled back. "Don't tell me to shut up, Cross."

"That's the least of what I'll tell you. And the whole damned world."

"It won't do you a damned bit of good," Mason growled. "You can't prove a thing. It's your word against mine." He clutched the briefcase to his expansive girth tightly. "Now," he added with a satisfied smile.

He turned and started lumbering toward the door, pushing Megan out of the way, sending her careening into the edge of the desk. An angry exclamation broke from Harlan Spencer, and he stepped quickly into the room. But Dev was quicker, leaping forward as if he'd never been injured. Mason never even saw the senator before Dev grabbed the fat man's shirt and, despite his great bulk, yanked him forward as if he were a lightweight.

"Don't you *ever,*" he ground out, "lay a hand on her again." He glanced over his shoulder at Megan. "Are you all right?"

The big man moved suddenly then, shoving at Dev and jerking away. Already wobbly, Dev reeled back. Megan leapt forward, long, slender fingers curling into claws, her obvious intention to slash out at Mason.

Mason whirled toward the door, but stopped dead when, for the first time, he saw the grim-faced Harlan Spencer. Dev reached for Megan's arm, halting her instinctive attack.

"Harlan," Mason said, recovering quickly and gesturing at Dev, "you won't believe what he's accusing me of! The man's crazy!"

"That's enough, Frank," Harlan said coldly. "I think you're in enough trouble already."

"*Me?* He's the one who—"

"Ordered number-five rivets instead of eights, to save a few bucks?" Dev cut in, his voice taut with pain and anger. "Increased the centers for the concrete reinforcement to save on the rebar, and to hell with weakening the whole structure? And how about that order for flyash? How much did that save you?"

"How did you— You can't prove that!"

Dev smiled tightly. "I wasn't sure of it . . . until now."

Mason swore, glaring at Dev. "You son of a—"

"Be quiet," Harlan said sharply. "I want to hear the rest of this."

Dev shuddered, his arm tightening against his injured side. He swayed on his feet. Megan tried to get him to sit down, but the best she could do was get him to lean against the desk.

"Go on, Dev. What's this about flyash?"

"It's an old trick," Dev said, "to substitute flyash for cement—about every fifth sack, maybe—nobody knows the difference from just seeing it. It looks the same, feels the same, sets up the same. Except that it's inherently weaker."

He glanced at the fuming Mason, then turned back to Harlan. "We wouldn't find out," Dev said grimly, "until a core sample was taken. Probably after the damned building had collapsed."

"That's absurd! It would never collapse from that!"

"Not from the weak concrete alone," Dev agreed wearily, "but add less reinforcement, smaller rivets..."

"Is the potential for disaster here as strong as I'm beginning to think it is?" Harlan asked.

Dev blinked, his eyes beginning to look a little glassy. He was swaying again, and Megan tightened her grip on his arm.

"Yes," he said at last, the words sounding too careful, as if he were having to concentrate very hard to get them out. "I think it is."

"That's bull—"

"I'd suggest you shut up, Frank," Harlan said abruptly. "You'll have enough explaining to do before this is over. And out of respect for our friendship, I'd recommend you find a good lawyer. Fast."

Mason seemed to crumple, all the bluster draining away. He sagged against the wall of the trailer, looking utterly defeated.

"You don't understand," he said dully. "I *had* to do it. I promised my backers we'd be in on time and under budget. That they'd have their return early. It was the only way I could raise the money to do it this way, with your damned park instead of the private golf course they wanted."

"So you were willing to risk hundreds of innocent lives," Harlan said harshly.

"It might not have ever happened. It could have held for years."

Harlan made a disgusted sound. He turned back to Dev, but with one look at the younger man's ashen face, he stopped whatever he'd been about to say.

"Dev," Megan said anxiously, worried by his growing unsteadiness, and by the sudden shallowness of his breathing, "you have to get back to the hospital—"

"No!"

Megan jumped at the vehement exclamation. "But you're hurt, you shouldn't have checked out, you need to be where they can take care of you."

"No," he said, less fervid now, but whether it was because he was calmer, or because he was weakening, Megan wasn't sure. "I'll...just...sit down...for a minute."

He got to his feet and turned as if to head for the chair behind the desk. On his second step, he let out a soft, muffled "Damn," and then slid limply to the floor.

Megan sat curled up in the big chair in the darkened room, watching the man in the bed, who was sleeping peacefully at last. He'd been restless at first, thrashing, even coming half-awake with a startled groan once.

"Shhh," she'd soothed him, laying a cool, slender hand on his brow. "It's all right, Dev."

"Meggie?" His voice had been hoarse, disbelieving.

"Of course," she whispered. "I'll be right here."

He'd slipped into sleep once more, quietly then, and when Megan awoke from a light doze to find him lying, not flat on his back but curled on his side with his head buried into the pillow, she knew he was at last getting the restful, healing sleep he needed.

"I know he should go back to the hospital," she'd said to her father when they'd brought him home, "but..."

"I know," Harlan had replied. "There's probably nothing he'd hate more. We'll call the doctor to find out what we should do for him."

Megan had tucked Dev into bed with all the tenderness of a devoted lover. And had refused to leave his side, hour after hour. Her father had watched her, an odd look crossing his face, but he'd said nothing.

When Harlan came in to check on her some time after that, she glanced at her watch, surprised to see that it was early afternoon. Several hours had passed since she and her father had half carried the slumping Dev out to the car, then into the house. She got to her feet, stretching muscles cramped from those hours of sitting. As Megan moved to stand by the bed, her father unexpectedly put an arm around her.

"You still love him, don't you?"

Megan raised her head and met her father's eyes steadily. "Yes," she said, unhesitatingly.

Harlan smiled. "You know, this may not be a very fatherly thing to say, but I think I'm glad. I've been so worried about you, baby. I was afraid you'd never find anyone to break through that shell you'd put around yourself."

He glanced at Dev, then back to her. "I never thought I'd forgive the man who hurt you so...but he's a good man, Megan, despite what happened between you before. It took a lot of guts to stand up to Frank that way."

"I know," Megan said softly.

Her father was a truly remarkable man, she thought. He'd been father and mother to her since she'd been fifteen, and had learned to cope with the vagaries of a teenage girl with the same aplomb that enabled him to handle the political infighting that came with his position. And if he'd been a little tough on her at times, it was only because he loved her. Of all the sins of all the parents she'd known and heard about, she could think of a lot worse than a little overprotectiveness.

"Meggie?"

The husky whisper snapped her out of her thoughts. She moved quickly to sit on the edge of the bed.

"Right here, love."

The hazel eyes were open, but looking a little dazed as he glanced around the room and startled when he saw her father there. "Where...?"

"My house."

He squeezed his eyes shut and moved his head as if he were trying to clear it. A grunt of pain broke from him at the movement. His hand lifted to the bandage on his head, then fell back.

"Just relax," she urged. "You need rest, Dev."

His eyes snapped open. "Mason."

Megan glanced over her shoulder at her father.

"He's in custody," Harlan said. "With a lot of explaining to do." He shook his head. "I shouldn't have doubted you, son. I should have realized Frank was in trouble. I suppose I just didn't want to see it. Amazing how blind we can be, when it's something so close to us."

"I know," Dev said quietly, his voice stronger now as he met Harlan's gaze unflinchingly. "I didn't want to think about Meg being pregnant, either."

Meg blushed, but respect flashed in Harlan's eyes. "I can't condone what you did," he said. "But given the horrible circumstances, I understand. And it took courage to admit that, especially to me."

Dev's mouth twisted in a wry smile. "Yes," he admitted ruefully. "It did. Almost more than I had."

Harlan looked at him for a moment, then nodded, and Megan knew it was at much more than Dev's words. Then her father tactfully left them alone.

Dev was quiet for a moment. Then, "Why did you bring me here?"

Megan took a deep breath. "Where else would I take the man I love?"

Dev's eyes widened. "The . . . what?"

He sounded like a little boy who didn't quite believe in an unexpected treasure on Christmas morning, and Megan's heart twisted inside her.

"I love you," she said softly.

"Oh, God, Meggie . . . even after what I did?"

"Let's put it behind us, Dev. We have a second chance." She reached out to gently touch the bruise on his cheek. "One we very nearly didn't get. Let's not waste it."

"Can you really forgive me? I deserted you. I ruined your dreams—"

"And you gave me Kevin," she said softly. Dev's breath caught. "I love you, Dev. I think I always did, even when I was trying so hard to hate you. I must have—why else would I have chosen to have your son and keep him?"

"*Our* son," Dev echoed, still not used to it.

"If you want . . ." she began, then trailed off, afraid to hope, afraid to believe.

"If I want?" His words came out in an incredulous rush. "*If* I want? Lord, Meg, there's nothing I want more in this world. Nothing."

"Then . . . you can forgive me? For not telling you?"

"I understand, Meg." His lips tightened. "Lord knows, you had no reason to trust me. Especially with something so precious."

Megan let out a breath she hadn't even been aware of holding. But it caught again as fear flashed across Dev's face, much as it had her own.

"What about Kevin?"

"I wouldn't worry about that," Megan said dryly. "You're all I've heard about for days. He thinks you're quite wonderful." She smiled suddenly, a tender, loving smile. "He's right, of course. As you said, he's a smart kid."

That smile lit a small, warm fire deep inside him. "Marry me, Meggie. I don't want to go another day without you, and my son."

The words came quickly, urgently, with a touch of wistfulness that made her lips curve into a soft, sweet smile. "I love you," she repeated fervently.

Dev pulled her down beside him, heedless of his battered ribs. "Does that mean yes?"

"Yes. Yes, yes and yes."

"You're sure? No doubts? I know I'll have to prove you can trust me—"

"No doubts," she said firmly, lifting her head to meet his wondering gaze. "That's all behind us. Remember?"

He let out a long breath. "I remember. I just may need help to keep on remembering."

"I'll help you."

He hugged her to him, lifting one hand to stroke her hair. They lay quietly together for a long time, just savoring the closeness. Megan snuggled closer, nuzzling his neck. He could feel her soft breath on his skin, the soft curves of her body pressing against him.

"Meg?"

"Hmm?"

"There's something else you could help me with."

"What?"

He turned his head and whispered into her ear. Megan blushed, then giggled.

"Dev! With my father in the house? Besides, you're hurt."

"Not that hurt. And I got the impression your father wouldn't be surprised to find that door locked." When she hesitated, he spoke softly. "We need this, Meg. I can't explain it, but..."

Without a word Megan uncurled gracefully from the bed, and Dev watched her as she crossed the room to lock the door. Even at that distance he could see her hands trembling, and doubt suddenly flooded him. Was she still uncertain, not sure of him, or was it her own feelings she didn't trust?

Then she came back, stopping beside the bed to slip off her clothes. Her hands were still trembling, but all of Dev's doubts had vanished. He could see her face now, could see the hot, vital desire glowing in her eyes, and knew with a rising joy that it was need, and anticipation, that was making her quiver.

As it was making him quiver, so fiercely that he had to tighten every muscle to control it. His aching ribs sent him a sharp reminder, but it was lost in the deluge of sensation as Megan stood naked before him.

She moved as if to return to the bed, then stopped. A soft, sensual smile curved her mouth as she reached up to the smooth coil of hair at the back of her head. Dev smothered a groan as the movement made her breasts sway gently, temptingly. Then she shook her head, and the honey-gold silk of her hair tumbled down around her shoulders.

"Meggie . . ."

It was low, soft and reverent. It made Megan's knees weak. And it told her that she'd been wrong, very wrong. Meggie wasn't gone, she'd only been in hiding, waiting for this man to come back.

She sank down on the bed, careful to avoid Dev's battered side as she stretched out beside him. Dev seemed to have no such concern, however; he pulled her close and began to press soft, sweet kisses on every part of her he could reach. She felt him wince as his bruised side protested, but he never slowed the tender yet blazing caress of his mouth over her skin.

It was up to her, she realized, to keep him from hurting himself; Dev had clearly thrown caution and care to the Santa Ana winds. She lifted herself up on one elbow.

"I think," she said, her voice low and husky as she gently touched the strapping around his ribs, "I'd better handle this."

Dev let out a low breath. "Handle anything you want."

"I'd rather handle what *you* want." Megan felt herself blush, but couldn't help smiling at Dev's heartfelt groan. "Tell me," she urged.

"Just touch me, Meggie. Anywhere. Everywhere. It's been forever." He sucked in a breath as her fingers brushed over his chest above the binding cloth, pausing only to tease the tightening disks of his nipples. "God, for so long I thought it would never..."

"It will be forever," she corrected him softly. She bent to him then, following the path her fingers had traced with her tongue. When she stroked and tasted his nipples, she felt him move beneath her, reach for her. "Let me," she whispered, restraining him. "Just let me do it all."

With a throttled groan, Dev fell back against the pillows, arms spread in an attitude that left Megan no doubts that he was hers to do with as she pleased. The thought thrilled her. She would take a long time, she promised herself, imprinting Devlin Cross so thoroughly on her mind and body that he would be as much a part of her as the heart he already owned.

She set about her task, touching, stroking, tasting, exploring, until she knew every inch of him, until she'd done things she had only dreamed about, until his heated and unequivocal response to her ministrations had her own body crying out with need.

Then Dev broke. "Please, Meggie. God, please now, I can't wait anymore."

"Neither can I," Megan said, barely aware of the way her voice sounded, low and harsh with her own urgency. With his hands on her hips to steady her, she straddled him, a thrill of anticipation rippling through her as she saw the fullness, the hardness of his body, more than ready for her. She reached for him, curling her fingers around him to guide him home.

"I love you, Meg," Dev said suddenly, urgently, as if it were somehow imperative that he say it now, before he was buried in her silken heat and lost to all but the incredible feelings they gave each other.

"I know you do," Megan answered, knowing instinctively that this was the reassurance he needed, much more than her returning the vow.

And then Dev was moving despite her efforts to keep him still. His hips arched upward, driving himself in deep, and Megan gasped, the pleasure of his sudden, thick invasion demanding the outlet of her choked cry. When he lowered himself to the bed again, Megan rode him down, savoring the movement, the feel of him hard and hot within her.

He was right, she thought as her body clenched, grasping at him, this was what they'd needed, these moments the purest and most wondrous in life, thrown back in the face of death. This was their ode to existence, their acknowledgment that the best defense against the ugliness of death was a life lived well and joyously.

And in the moment when she saw Dev's face go taut, when he cried out her name, sharp and sweet, when he gripped her tightly as his hips jerked and he erupted within her in hot, heavy beats, when the pleasure he found with her honed his face to pure, male beauty, Megan knew that she was truly free of all the hurt and pain of the past. She'd found again the one man, the only man for her, the father of her child, and of the rest of her children to come. She'd found him again, and this time she would hold him forever. With a passionate cry of his name, she ground her body against his one last time, and went flying after him.

Epilogue

Harlan Spencer was pacing the room restlessly, his hair looking uncharacteristically ruffled. The reason became clear when he lifted a hand to run it anxiously through the silver strands. He glanced at his watch, then at the wall clock as if he didn't believe what his own watch had told him, and resumed his pacing.

At last a door swung open, and he whirled to see an even more disheveled Dev, looking haggard and drained in the baggy green clothing. Harlan crossed to him in two long strides, grabbing his shoulders.

"Megan?"

"She's all right." He shuddered. "As much as anyone could be, after that."

Harlan relaxed a little, releasing him. "I've always said if the future of the human race was left up to the men, we wouldn't be here now," he said. "Well?"

Dev shoved a lock of sweat-dampened hair back off his forehead. Then he looked up at his father-in-law and grinned.

"A girl. The second most beautiful female in the world."

Harlan's solemn face split into a wide grin. "A girl. Kevin's got a baby sister. I'll be damned."

"I doubt that."

Harlan started to reach for Dev's shoulder, then stopped and hugged him fiercely instead.

"I'm proud of both of you," he said earnestly.

"Thank you." Dev returned the hearty embrace. "But Meg did all the work. All I did was coach." He glanced at the clock. "She should be in her room by now. Let's go see her." He grinned at Harlan. "Then we'll go get Kevin and I'll introduce you to your granddaughter."

Megan looked tired, a little pale, but the joyous smile that lit her face when they came in made it unimportant. She lifted a hand to Dev, the other to her father.

"Oh, Daddy, she's beautiful! Have you seen her yet?"

"Not yet, baby. We'll be on our way there, after we pick up Kevin from the hospital playroom, but I wanted to see *my* little girl first." He squeezed her hand. "You're sure you're all right?"

"Yes. It was hard, but—" she looked at Dev "—Dev was there."

"Yeah," her husband said wryly, "and I was a lot of help, too. I damned near passed out the first time you screamed."

Megan smiled. "Instead you apologized every five minutes for making me pregnant."

"I apologized," he corrected with a wicked grin, "for it having to hurt you so much. I have no intention of apologizing for all the fun we had getting you that way."

"Dev!" Megan blushed as her father chuckled.

"Especially," Dev went on, his voice suddenly low, quiet and filled with love, "since it produced such a beautiful child."

"Yes," Megan said, "she is. So beautiful." Her eyes went to her father, then back to Dev. He caught her hint, nodded and turned to Harlan.

"With your permission," he said formally, "we'd like to name her Catherine."

Harlan took a quick breath, then blinked rapidly. He looked from Dev to Megan, his eyes suspiciously bright. "Thank you. Both of you." He squeezed his daughter's hand once more. "Your mother would be so proud."

"I hope so, Daddy." Megan looked up at Dev. "And if *you* don't mind," she said softly, "I'd like her middle name to be Elizabeth."

Dev stared at her, his eyes going wide with shock. "Meg, I—"

"Please? If not because she was your wife, or because she died much too young...then because she was your best friend?"

"Ah, Meggie..." He gently pulled her hand up to his lips and kissed it. "I love you."

And later, when Megan's father had taken Kevin—too adult at nearly ten to be *truly* worried, yet reassured now that he had seen his mother was all right—to the nursery to see the tiny miracle, Dev sat on the edge of the bed and again kissed his wife's hand, right over the gold band on her left ring finger.

"I brought you something."

"What?" she asked. "Besides love, joy, the sweetest four years of my life and the most precious little boy and girl in the world?"

Dev flushed slightly. "Thank you," he said huskily, pulling a large envelope out of his pocket, "but this is what I meant."

She opened it, and gasped at the sight of the parchment that slid out.

"The school said they were sorry you had to miss the ceremony. But under the circumstances, they understood."

Megan stared at the degree inscribed in elegant Roman script. At long last, her degree in fine arts. She didn't quite believe it. She had gone back to school five weeks after their wedding, after Dev had quietly but firmly faced down her father.

"She deserves this chance, sir," he'd said respectfully, "if for no other reason than that it's what she wants. What she always wanted. That's enough for me."

Her father, surprisingly, had buckled without a fight. "You shame me, Dev. You're right. And you're right for my little girl."

It had been the beginning of a new relationship between all of them, and the beginning of the busiest, yet happiest time of Megan's life. After, of course, the sweet, passion-filled month they'd spent in the Bahamas on the honeymoon that had been a gift from her father. They were a family now; Dev and Kevin had rapidly made up for lost time, her father and Dev were becoming closer every day... and now the newest miracle, the sunny-haired, hazel-eyed little girl who was the symbol of all they'd won.

"I've really got it," she murmured in wonder, staring down at the precious paper.

"That," Dev said with an exaggerated leer, "is the understatement of the century."

Megan threw her arms around him and hugged him fiercely. "I love you. So much. I've never been so happy."

"I didn't think I could ever be this happy." He hugged her back, stroking the long, silken braid of her hair. "You saved my life ten years ago, Meggie. It nearly killed me to walk away from you. And after I did, you had every right to make me pay for it. But instead, you gave me my life back again. I love you, Meggie. I'll love you forever."

And as he held her in his arms, he knew it was nothing less than the truth.

* * * * *

SPRING FANCY

Three bachelors, footloose
and fancy-free... until now!

Spring into romance with three
fabulous fancies by three of
Silhouette's hottest authors:

ANNETTE BROADRICK
LASS SMALL
KASEY MICHAELS

When spring fancy strikes, no man is immune!

Look for this exciting new short-story collection
in March at your favorite retail outlet.

Only from

Silhouette®

where passion lives.

Silhouette Books
is proud to present
our best authors,
their best books...
and the best in
your reading pleasure!

Throughout 1993, look for exciting books
by these top names in contemporary
romance:

CATHERINE COULTER—
Aftershocks in February

FERN MICHAELS—
Nightstar in March

DIANA PALMER—
Heather's Song in March

ELIZABETH LOWELL
Love Song for a Raven in April

SANDRA BROWN
(previously published under
the pseudonym Erin St. Claire)—
Led Astray in April

LINDA HOWARD—
All That Glitters in May

When it comes to passion,
we wrote the book.

Silhouette®   BOBT1RR

NORA ROBERTS

Love has a language all its own, and for centuries flowers have symbolized love's finest expression. Discover the language of flowers—and love—in this romantic collection of 48 favorite books by bestselling author Nora Roberts.

Two titles are available each month at your favorite retail outlet.

In March, look for:

The Art of Deception, Volume #27
Untamed, Volume #28

In April, look for:

Dual Image, Volume #29
Second Nature, Volume #30

Collect all 48 titles
and become fluent in

THE LANGUAGE of LOVE

Silhouette®

SILHOUETTE® *Desire*

HAWK'S WAY

HAWK'S WAY—where the Whitelaws of Texas run free till passion brands their hearts. A hot new series from Joan Johnston!

Look for the first of a long line of Texan adventures, beginning in April with THE RANCHER AND THE RUNAWAY BRIDE (D #779), as Tate Whitelaw battles her bossy brothers—and a sexy rancher.

Next, in May, Faron Whitelaw meets his match in THE COWBOY AND THE PRINCESS (D #785).

Finally, in June, Garth Whitelaw shows you just how hot the summer can get in THE WRANGLER AND THE RICH GIRL (D #791).

Join the Whitelaws as they saunter about HAWK'S WAY looking for their perfect mates . . . only from Silhouette Desire!

SDHW1